Parallel Lives

Richard Seltzer

Parallel Lives

Copyright © 2020 by Richard Seltzer

ISBN 13: 978-1-7346855-0-3

Library of Congress Control Number: 2020933937

Cover Photos: Photo by Victor Freitas on Unsplash

Cover design © by All Things That Matter Press
Published in 2020 by All Things That Matter Press

Dedication

To my wife Barbara (Babs), 1950-2012

Acknowledgements

Rochelle Cohen for her frequent helpful feedback and encouragement.
My son Bob for his continuing support.
My mother, Helen, who endured Alzheimer's, 1920-2010
My father, Dick, who suffered a stroke, 1923-2014
My sister, Raven, the acupuncturist
Elizabeth Warren, who I wish had become the first woman president

1 ~ The Place Where Time Stopped

Because of the remoteness of the place and its elevation, Abe felt like a newcomer to Thomas Mann's *Magic Mountain.* Here was a world apart, totally separate from the city-life he was used to. But he wasn't a young man, nor were the other residents. They hadn't come here to be cured. There was no cure for what they had, and they didn't delude themselves that they would ever move from here to another earthly dwelling. This was the end of the road. They were old and would only get older. They were here to enjoy what was left of life; ideally, to figure out what life was about before it ended, and to do so in deliberate isolation from family and friends. That was the attraction of this remote location. They were on their own. Here they would not become the children of their children, dependent on them, pulled hither and thither to deal with family and social obligations, distracted at a time when time was running out, when they needed quiet and leisure to find their center, if there was a center, to find meaning if there were meaning.

Perhaps it was unrealistic to have such hopes when first arriving at an assisted-living facility. And perhaps preparing for the move was a form of evasion and self-delusion. His wife, Babs, had died three years ago. As Abe came out of the fog of grief and depression, he had focused his energies on dealing with the practical matters that had to be dealt with—organizing his resources and reducing his recurring expenses, divesting himself of hundreds of boxes filled with the relics of a lifetime. Then he had researched, online, the facilities that were in his price range and that were sufficiently remote for his purposes. But focusing on the means to his end had been a way to avoid thinking about the end itself, both in the sense of a goal and in the sense of end of life, which must inevitably come, whether sooner or later, and which had come much too soon for Babs. This would be so different if she were here with him. No, together they would never have made this choice.

***

As the Uber from the bus station maneuvered along the winding road through the snow-covered peaks of the White Mountains, Abe realized his perspective was now far different than it would have been fifty years before. Then, he would have fantasized about the nearby ski slopes—the rush he got from the cold wind in his face, the mixture of control and speed, the inevitability of descent balanced by the freedom to choose which way to go, and to change his mind repeatedly.

He would spend the rest of his days here in ski country, but he'd never ski again. It wasn't just a matter of physical agility. He had no desire for such activity. Time was short. He believed that life was an adventure that he could only experience once. And, he wanted to experience the end of it to the fullest he was capable of, with eyes open, in hope that there could be a moment when the pieces came together and his life made and the world made sense.

Dante was doubly lucky—he had his revelation in the middle of his life. And he started with a structure of ideas that he and those around him shared. For Dante, revelation was a matter of recognizing the connections between that structure and his life and the lives of everyone he knew or had heard of.

Abe had no such faith, neither from religion nor philosophy. Without a map, he hoped to get to his destination without knowing what or where that destination was or even if there was one. Ever the optimist, he hoped to have his personal revelation while he still had the capacity to understand, much less to savor such a moment, before the onset of the darkness of memory loss— his greatest fear, worse than death.

The ragged face of the Old Man of the Mountains came into view. One moment the rocks formed a face—rough, but with mythic power, resonating in the imagination. Then, after the next twist of the road, they were just random rocks. It was a trick of perspective. The experience of the face appearing and disappearing and then appearing again was like an optical illusion involving a shift between foreground and background. Now you see a vase. Now you see two faces. He thought of the classic black and white image of yin and yang, the light defined by the darkness and the darkness by the light with the pairs of opposites dependent on one another. One and zero. Yes and no. On and off. Free will and determination. Randomness and meaning. Maybe all that was required for a moment of revelation was a change of perspective. Maybe moving here was the change he needed.

Maybe he already knew the answers to questions about the meaning of life. Maybe he had known since birth; but he didn't know the questions so he didn't realize the answers were answers. A cosmic joke. 42 in the *Hitch Hiker's Guide to the Galaxy*. Random and arbitrary was the nature of the universe.

Abe pulled out his cellphone, from habit, to check the time, the weather, and the news; it was dead. The phone was fully charged. He was sure of that. But the screen was blank and pressing buttons didn't bring it back to life.

He knew that cellphones were prohibited at this facility. It wasn't just assisted living, this was set up as a retreat, a place where residents could get away from the world that had been too much with them, late and soon. He expected that. He wanted that.

Maybe the phone was dead from a mechanical problem. Maybe when it was in his pocket he had banged it against something without noticing. Or maybe the latest software update had brought this on.

He had thought that he was ready to give up his connection to the outside world, but he hadn't realized how much he depended on it. His phone was an extension of his nervous system. Checking his phone was as natural and necessary as breathing. He hadn't realized how visceral his dependence on it was when he decided to move somewhere where he'd have to give that up. Maybe this move was a mistake. He should tell the driver to turn around and take him back.

Then around the next bend he saw it. White clapboard, but pinkish from the sunset, like the snow around it and halfway up a medium-size mountain, about 2000 feet above the highway that meandered below — his new home, the beginning of the rest of his life.

The car strained on the steep slope and slipped twice on patches of ice. When they reached the visitors' parking lot in front of the main building, Abe once again saw the Old Man of the Mountains, the Great Stone Face that Hawthorne had written about. From here he saw it as a man, majestic and grand, and not as random rocks. He took that as a good omen.

Yes, he would go ahead. He wouldn't turn back. He'd make what he could of the new life ahead of him. It was time to shuffle the deck and deal the cards of fate. The eternal miracle: a random shuffle determining fate. Is anything random? he thought. Is there fate? Or are randomness and fate inseparable, like yin and yang?

Abe had read dozens of brochures, had watched dozens online promotional videos and had decided that it was here at Arcadia Estates that he would start afresh. He wasn't a seventeen-year-old falling in love with a girl at first sight. He was a seventy-year-old falling in love with a structure and a way of life without visiting, without even speaking to residents.

By nature, Abe was deliberate and cautious, at least during his married life, when every decision affected not just him, but his wife and two kids, as well. Meeting Babs had been different. He knew immediately, felt in his gut that she was the one. And now she was gone, he once again trusted his gut, and was willing to gamble his remaining life on impulse

In photos, Arcadia Estates had reminded him of a once fashionable hotel in Plymouth, New Hampshire, where he had grown up. Pemigewasset House was torn down to make way for a college dormitory soon after his family moved to town, when he was in the seventh grade. It was named for the Indian tribe that had lived nearby and that had given its name to the river as well. That was where Nathaniel Hawthorne died in 1864 while visiting with former president Franklin Pierce. Even after it was replaced by the dormitory, Abe had felt a ghostly presence about the property, knowing that a great author had once walked there.

He dreaded entering this new world but had no choice. Since the sudden death of Babs, daily life, alone had become a series of chores that he dreaded and did poorly, if he remembered to do them at all. He was living in squalor and was malnourished and lethargic, stumbling from one day to the next, with no schedule, nothing that needed to be done, and no one he had to interact with. He was virtually dead, and if he continued that way much longer, he'd be literally dead as well.

The price for assisted living was ridiculously high, but he could afford it with the sale of his house, the end of all the recurrent costs of house, and car ownership, and independent living. The house sale yielded far less than he had expected. He had unwittingly let the house deteriorate after Babs died. But, combined with Social Security, and his 401K, he could afford Arcadia. He had simple tastes, and the assisted living would take care of all necessities. And if and when his physical condition deteriorated to the point where he could no longer take care of himself, he was guaranteed a spot in the next lower circle of Hell, where support and care were available 24/7. And should the worst happen, Alzheimer's or some other mental or memory breakdown, he was guaranteed that kind of care as well, behind a locked door where he would be guaranteed the right to "a world of his own."

So first he would have to adapt from the lifestyle of a hermit to enforced and scheduled sociability. He'd eat three nutritious meals and one snack at regular hours in company with hundreds of others. Never again would he have to buy groceries and cook or wash dishes or do laundry, or even vacuum his apartment. This many-faceted assistance would free up hours, enabling him to participate in a wide range of communal activities or to pursue personal projects, if he had personal projects, giving him the gift of time and then relieving him of the chore of deciding what to do with it.

Stepping out of the car and surveying the rambling structure that would be his new home, Abe savored hints of the past overlaid on the present. He got that sensation all too rarely in today's suburbs, with the same chain stores and gas stations everywhere. Far too many assisted-living facilities were cookie-cutter modern, designed for efficiency in heating and cooling and for packing as many residents as possible into the given space.

This facility consisted of a series of Victorian houses that had been added to repeatedly for pragmatic rather than aesthetic reasons. He knew that sheltered passageways connected the buildings, and elevators connected the floors, so there was never a need for a resident to don a coat and boots and venture into the snow, and those in wheelchairs could easily go anywhere on the premises.

Back in the 1850s, the buildings had been a cluster of individual homes, a tiny village. Soon before the First World War, they were bought up and converted into an exclusive boarding school for girls.

With the decline in popularity of single-sex schools after the Viet Nam War, the property was sold again and converted into a nursing home.

An extensive library, a relic of the defunct school, had been retained as an impressive attraction for would-be residents. But declining eyesight and diminished attention-spans made reading far less enjoyable in actuality than in prospect.

Attached to the main building was what was once a barn and carriage house. The downstairs had stalls for two horses and space for carriage and sleigh. Hay was stored upstairs in a spacious loft. The girls' school transformed the loft into an auditorium and gym with a stage and basketball court. It now served as an "activity room" for community meetings, seasonal celebrations, musical performances, and Sunday church services.

Legend had it that the clock on the cupola atop that loft had stopped at the stroke of midnight when the original owner's wife died. Neighbors suspected he broke the clock himself and reset it to the time of her death. In any case, subsequent owners honored the tradition and didn't have it repaired, so the house came to be known as "the place where time stopped."

Standing in the parking lot, with his suitcases beside him, little did Abe suspect that this was the beginning of adventure, romance, danger and revelation such as he had never dreamed possible.

2 ~ First night

Abe had missed dinner, which was served at 4:30. Who the hell eats supper at 4:30 in the afternoon? he wondered. He was used to cooking for himself at eight or nine.

That was one of the aspects of communal living he wasn't looking forward to—the daily schedule, adapted to the needs and wishes of the majority and for the convenience of the staff. Most of these folks would probably be in bed by seven.

The lady on duty at reception, Melody according to her name tag, got him a ham sandwich, chips, and a diet Coke from the kitchen. He was happy to put off meeting other residents and adjusting to their fixed schedule. Tonight, he would relax in solitude in his new apartment.

Abe's unit was furnished. Many prospective residents didn't want to haul furniture up a mountain in the middle of nowhere. That suited Abe fine. He didn't want to bring anything from his past except his clothes. He wanted no reminders, except a few photos of Babs, two of which he hung in the bedroom so he could see them as he lay in bed at night; and one that he put on the end-table next to the sofa in the living room.

He would savor this last opportunity to be on his own schedule, to do whatever he wanted, whenever he wanted, the hermit-like freedom he was giving up by moving here.

He had brought his "desert island" collection of books that were worthy of multiple rereading including *Ulysses*, *Finnegan's Wake*, *The Brothers Karamazov*, *The Magic Mountain*, *The Magus*, Durant's *Story of Civilization*, and *The King James Bible*. He stacked the books on the end table by the recliner, turned the three-way floor lamp to its highest, polished the lenses of his reading glasses, and prepared for hours of escape.

He read a page of one, then two pages of another, then opened and closed half a dozen more. Nothing caught his attention. He began to wonder, Do I really want to read now? Am I ever likely to read these books? Who am I trying to impress? Myself? No one else was likely to know if he did or didn't read them. But if he didn't read them, he wasn't sure what else he'd do.

He asked himself, Why the hell am I here alone, in the middle of nowhere? Will my days just be filled with organized group activities?

He deliberately hadn't brought a TV. And the rules prohibited computers, just as they did cellphones. But there were communal TVs in public rooms, and he could easily fall into the habit of staring at nonsense in company with zombie-like old people with walkers and wheelchairs. What a fate!

Abe was tired. His eyes were tired. That's why he couldn't concentrate. It had been a long day. Despite the early hour, he should turn in. Everything would look better in the morning.

Before going to bed, he stopped by the housekeeping supply room to pick up an extra pillow. He couldn't sleep at night without that weight on his right shoulder, where Babs's head should have been.

He went through his usual routine, including a hot bath and a cup of hot tea. Then he stretched out on his back, the pillow in place, and relaxed one body part after another, and started counting, silently. If he became aware of an awkwardness in his position—a discomfort, an itch—he'd deal with that, then start counting again. This routine had worked every night since Babs died. He'd fall asleep before he counted to a hundred. And when he woke up two or three times during the night, needing to urinate, he'd go through this routine again, and once again smoothly and predictably fall asleep.

He considered the frequent waking as a benefit, rather than an affliction of age. He woke with images of his dreams fresh in his mind, dreams that he would have otherwise forgotten.

Sometimes before going back to sleep, he would sit on the edge of his bed, relax, and let the dream images once again flow through his mind; sometimes, like meditation, they would give him a feeling of contentment, at peace with himself and in touch with his unconscious. Often his dreams included images from his childhood and from his life with Babs, reshuffled and from different perspectives, seeing himself and others as viewed by someone else. Sometimes these were in familiar settings, but often in houses and cities he had no memory of in his conscious life, though they might recur, night after night, providing an element of continuity in an otherwise random sequence of images.

But perhaps there was an underlying logic that determined what he saw and when. He was reminded of computer-based synchronizing of sounds with colors, shapes, and motions. He remembered outdoor shows on cruise ships, where a fountain pulsed in rhythm with the music, and colored lights flashed on the water also in sync with the music.

The pillow became Babs's head. They cuddled. Their breathing was in sync. Their hearts beat in sync. And the white noise of the fan in the hot-air heating system became her voice recounting the day's crises and concerns. Though, in the telling, they lost their sting and became trivial and typical and amusing, no worse than a belly-ache from gas. This too shall pass, in the pass-fail system of life, as life is transformed in the telling, and irritants get transformed to pearls, and wisdom is both wise and dumb. The why is and was and always will be the toughest question; the quest and request, the test and retest; thought triggering thought, sensation triggering sensation, and images flashing, strobing, creating the movie-like illusion of movement and change. Everything was always there and only the light changed; the light and the watching her running across a field soon after sunset, the golfers having gone home, the course, of course, all hers, all ours alone together.

And Babs stretched out in a sand trap as if it were a sandy beach. Abe dove beside her and on top of her, and they rolled, clutching and feeling one another, close and clothes and less clothes and more skin and more touch and hands go where no hands have gone before, opening new worlds of sensation and memories indelible, fresh, always fresh flesh. Flesh to flesh, the true promise, not ashes to ashes. Asses to asses and tongues to tongues and fingertips everywhere— talking, discovering, understanding, in her standing, young love eternal.

A rustle of leaves in a stand of trees. The scramble to dress, to laugh, to run, hand-in-hand, freedom. Who needs words to speak?

Now I lay me not to speak. Now I lay you. Now you lay me. Lay men and lay women in the church of love.

She tripped. He grabbed her to stop her from falling, and tripped himself, legs scrambling to find his balance; but no ground, no ground at all—groundless, falling, feet thrashing in mid-air.

Abe woke with an urgent need to urinate and rushed to the toilet where his mind replayed the images he had just felt. In the replay he noticed another presence just out of the range of sight, another voice saying other words, just out of the range of sound. A touch, a breath, a taste that wasn't Babs.

Disconcerting. A chill, a shiver, but not of fear, rather of anticipation, promises to keep. And the sand was snow, and the snow felt good, and they warmed one another, holding tight.

He was back in bed, once again holding the pillow, only the pillow wasn't Babs. Babs was gone, but the pillow was there, and the peripheral presence was there. He was warm and not alone, relaxed, and counting himself back to sleep.

When he woke and dressed in the morning, there was sand in his shoes. He had no idea where that could have come from.

3 ~ Just Abe and Lord Have Mercy

It was early, 6:30 a.m., far earlier than he normally got up. It was still dark outside; but having gone to bed so early, he was wide awake. Abe was proud of himself for being so full of energy on this the first full day of the rest of his life. Aside from night staff, he was probably the only person awake—the elderly residents would probably laze in bed until ten, eleven, or even noon.

Then he heard stampeding feet in the hallway. He opened the door and was caught in the rush to breakfast. He ducked to get out of the way of motorized wheelchairs. He was pushed against the hallway railing and then got in the way of people who needed to hold onto that railing to maintain their balance while they walked. He laughed at his foolishness. He regretted having left behind the comfortable solitary habits he had fallen into after Babs died. Better to have rotted there alone than here as part of a communal mob.

Despite himself, not sure where the dining room was and not yet hungry since he often skipped breakfast, he was caught in the flow of the traffic and carried along. 106. He needed to remember 106. Maybe he should keep a crib sheet in his pocket, with not just his apartment number, but his name as well in case he was to forget that, and maybe a note to remind himself of the meaning life. Oh, yes, he had already forgotten that.

Then he noticed a straggler, the only person left behind him in the hall. Her back was turned toward him as she leaned over, holding onto the railing, and took off her shoes, turned them upside down, and knocked them against the wall.

"How the hell did I get sand in my shoes?" she exclaimed to no one in particular.

"My sentiments exactly," Abe interjected. "Is that a common occurrence here?"

"Of course, this being a beach resort, we find sand everywhere."

Abe laughed, then she laughed, too.

"I'm Abe," he walked over and reached out his hand. "I just moved in yesterday."

"Mercy," she replied.

"And your name is?" he asked.

"Mercy, as in 'Lord have mercy.' That's what everyone calls me now, not Mary, my birth name. Mercy, an old variant of Mary. That's my brother Jemmie's name for me. I'm his sister of mercy, he says. And here everyone calls me that."

"I'm Abe, Abe Daly, just Abe, always have been."

"Pleased to meet you, Just Abe."

She had purple hair, and she was two or three inches shorter than him, so her hair was at his eye level. He couldn't help but stare at the hair rather than look her in the eye.

"Chemo sabe, like the Lone Ranger," she said with a smile, and lifted the wig, showing her bald skull. "When your hair goes, you're free to replace it with whatever you like. That's liberating. Great fun."

It was awkward to stare at her skull, so he looked in her eyes.

Looking back at him, her face lit up, echoes of Meg Ryan having aged decades since *Sleepless in Seattle*, but still stunning: a very interesting lady. Before this, Abe had assumed that he would never again meet an interesting lady.

She looked straight in his eyes, with no restraint.

The two of them stared at each other for what must have been less than a minute, but it felt like the final minute of the Super Bowl, with one lead-change after another.

"Shall we dance?" she suggested, taking his arm and leading him to the dining room.

The hallways, the dining room, the apartments, the entire facility had hardwood floors instead of carpet, making it easier for those in wheelchairs to get around.

The dining room had murals instead of wallpaper, probably dating back to the days of the girls' school. On all sides, Abe saw scenes from colonial days and the Revolution.

The room was crowded and noisy. With half a dozen wheelchairs in front of them, the buffet line was slow.

When they found seats at an empty table for six, Abe ventured to compliment Mercy, "I'm surprised to find someone so young as you a resident here. I would have guessed that you were staff."

"Well, I'm not all that young," she chuckled. "But I do serve as part-time staff for a reduction of rent. I teach chair yoga."

"Chair yoga?"

"Yes, exercise for those with limited mobility. It's a real thing, not a joke. And I do counselling when needed. I have an MA in psychology from NYU online. I also play piano for community events. On Sundays I hold a religious service in the activity room. Others do the Jewish, Catholic and generic Protestant services in the chapel. I'm an ordained pastor, having spent all of fifteen minutes filling out the form at the web site of the Universal Life Church. I do the service in my own way, making it up as I go along. I'm a talker, and it's fun having an audience and a fixed time each week for me to deliver my thoughts. I'll be doing that tomorrow morning. 10 a.m. I'll expect to see you there, now that we're old friends. I'm going to talk about seeing without looking."

When he gave her a puzzled look, she pulled a pencil out of her pocketbook, grabbed a doily from an empty place-setting and staring Abe in the eye, never glancing at the paper, drew an impressionistic, but recognizable likeness of him.

"How did you do that?"

"It's a right brain/left brain thing. Got it from a book called *Drawing with the Right Side of Your Brain.* That's one aspect of what I want to talk about tomorrow."

"That's amazing. Being able to draw like that, I can imagine the fun you must have had doing that with your kids."

"No kids."

"Sorry. It's just your manner. I thought you must have kids and grandkids or be a teacher of young kids. I shouldn't have presumed. Is that a sore spot?"

She looked him in the eye again, and it felt to Abe as if she looked through him. Then she smiled and launched into her back-story. "Bill was my first love. He was going to be my one and only. We thought it was love, at least I did. It was an unspoken assumption that we would get married after graduation. Senior year, when I found out I was pregnant, I wasn't surprised, and wasn't upset, either. Yes, there'd be the embarrassment of telling our parents, but they'd get over it. They wouldn't be surprised. They certainly suspected that we were sleeping together. They'd have probably been shocked if they heard that we weren't. And we wanted kids. I certainly did. So, I was shocked when the first thing he thought of was abortion. We didn't even discuss other options. He was pre-med. All too quickly he found out what needed to be done and where and what it would cost. This was before Roe vs. Wade, but abortion was legal in New York. He was proud that he could find the closest and most economical clinic. In the days before the Web, that wasn't an easy matter.

"We were at Penn State. I was going to continue there and get an MA in social work. He was going to go there for med school.

"When I came back from the abortion, he told me he was going to go to UCLA instead. And that was it. No talk of marriage. No talk of me going out there with him. We'd go on with our separate lives as if that were what we had intended to do all along. And without a baby in common, he had no obligation to me, no responsibility for me. It ended. I didn't know what to say or what to do. If he could end it like that, if he felt nothing for me, I wasn't going to plead and beg. It would have been torture to spend the rest of my life with someone who didn't love me.

"My mind was a blank. For weeks, I probably looked and acted like a zombie. But I didn't cry. And when I finally got a postcard from him from LA with some Xs and Os under the signature, I laughed, and felt relieved. I had dodged a bullet. I was damned lucky.

"I got my degree. I got a job as a case worker for Social Services in New York and I moved to Brooklyn.

"Fifteen years later, I met and married Frank. I wanted to have kids. The more time passed, the more I realized that. But I didn't want to do it alone. Single parenthood wasn't done in those days, not in middle-class America. It wasn't a choice to consider. And having been burnt so brutally by Bill, I was cautious. I dated a lot. I slept around a little. But I couldn't find the one, the one I could trust as well as love, the one who could be the father of my children—until Frank.

"We both wanted children, but it turned out that we couldn't. This was before the time of in vitro and all the modern ways of bypassing the body's inabilities. And Frank balked at the idea of adoption. So, we had each other and enjoyed each other, and it was a good life, until we were both diagnosed with cancer.

"His diagnosis came first, which led to my going to get checked. His was too far advanced—inoperable, incurable. Mine they got early. You could say his dying saved my life. That's what we told each other.

"His cancer came and went—multiple remissions. We thought he might survive for another year, maybe more. Then one morning I woke up with my head resting on the shoulder of a corpse."

"That must have been horrible."

"Oh, it was. It certainly was. But not as horrible as the funeral."

"The grief. I know what it's like to lose someone you love."

"This was worse. Believe me. We had picked a plot under an ancient oak tree that stood all alone on the top of a hill. We had plenty of time to shop around, to plan for the endgame, to get ready. But we couldn't plan the weather. A cloud burst, a thunderstorm.

"I hadn't wanted a crowd. Death was hard enough to deal with. I didn't want to have to play hostess to a mob at such a time. I hate funerals.

"It was just me, my brother Jemmie, and the pastor from our Congregational church.

"As the rain poured down, and while the pastor and I stood over the open grave, Jemmie took shelter under the oak tree. He was leaning against it when lightning struck. The doctors said it was a miracle he survived. But he wasn't the same after that, wasn't right in his mind. Underneath, he was the same old lovable and loving Jemmie, but he would slip back and forth between this reality and another one.

"The pastor saw it as a miracle in the religious sense rather than in the sense of a lucky medical accident. He was predisposed to that by his version of the liturgy, referring to the communion table as a portal to another reality.

"Well, Jemmie survived, but with severe damage to the left side of his brain. His editor, his censor, his ability to rationally explain the inexplicable no longer works. He's needed me since then. He's the child I never had—a rotund, always cheerful, seventy-year-old child.

"He's why I'm here. Yes, at a young age. Yes, please keep thinking it's a very young age, and I'll never say a word to contradict you. I need the help of 'assisted living' to keep the two of us going, and we enjoy the society, the togetherness with the new friends we've made here. And when Jemmie reaches the point of no return, he'll have a place here, where he can be taken care of.

"Sometimes Jemmie babbles nonsense. Other times his words provoke me to look at myself or others in a different way. I think of him as a 'holy fool'. Sometimes he retreats to his own world; then, when he comes back, he blesses me with what he found there. If he had been born at another time, in another culture, he might have become a shaman or a holy wandering pilgrim or a court jester. He has a way of getting me to take a second look at what I otherwise would take for granted, to recognize the extraordinary in the ordinary. He isn't just my brother James. He's my treasure, my gem, my Jemmie."

4 ~ A Tale of Two Minds

Why did I tell him so much so soon? Mercy wondered. That's not my style. I haven't shared that much with anyone else here, and I've been here for two years. Is there such a thing as sleep-talking? Saying whatever comes into your head because you haven't woken up, or because you were knocked out of your everyday pattern of thought by a chance encounter, and surprising yourself by acting and sounding like a different person than you are, than you have ever been? Maybe it's a right-brain/left-brain thing.

And what's his story? Shy. Uptight. Ring on his ring finger, but alone, obviously alone. A widower who is not yet finished grieving. I put my ring aside after three years. Maybe he's near that point.

Able bodied. Distinguished, not old. A Robert Redford look. Aging gracefully, sexily. But checking into a place like this, as if it were a monastery, as if his life were over. Giving up. Expecting nothing more of life. He probably has family and friends, but he prefers to be alone with his thoughts and his memories, rather than get caught up in their lives. He doesn't want to have to be bothered with the daily hassles of shopping and cooking and cleaning and the other tasks that assisted living takes care of. For him, it's a trade-off. He's willing to endure social contact in order to get those hassles taken care of. But he just wants to be alone This a man who has given up on life. A man who has chosen to exist rather than to live.

He certainly didn't expect to find the likes of me, to like someone like me. And he does like me. I have no doubt about that. He can't keep his eyes off me. That's refreshing, invigorating.

He's naive when it comes to women. Unselfconscious, with no control over his facial expressions. He hides nothing. He looks me straight in the eye, thinking only about what he's seeing, rather than being aware of what others are thinking of him, how they interpret his looks and gestures, as if all that he says is the words he speaks. How can he be so naive? How can he be that sweet? That's unexpected in a seventy-year old. He must have been very close to the wife who died. He must have needed no one else but her, and to have hidden nothing from her. He was so used to intimacy, he so depended on it, that he doesn't know how to function now that it's gone.

He has the emotional maturity of a teenager. Yes, that's appealing. But it's scary, too. He's vulnerable. If I show too much interest too soon, he's liable to go overboard and attach himself to me and become dependent on me. And that could be difficult to back out of in close quarters like these, where I couldn't help but bump into him; if I ever wanted to back out, which I might not.

Take it slow. Savor the moment. It's been all too long since I felt a tingle of anticipation in the presence of a man.

***

Slow down, Abe thought. This is a whirlwind of a woman. Way out of my league. I don't know what I'm getting myself into. I'm vulnerable, like in Joan Didion's *The Year of Magical Thinking*. It's been more than a year for me. The death of Babs, the shock of it left me expecting something wonderful and magical to balance that horror. Am I crazy enough to believe in love at first sight at the age of seventy; to believe in having a once-in-a-lifetime love a second time? Do I believe in fate, that fate is fair, and that it owes me one — a big one — and this woman could be it? I shouldn't hesitate. I should take the plunge and have faith in my instincts, throw away my reason like a teenager drunk on hormones and just flip a switch and become someone I've never been before.

Right brain left brain. Lame-brained. For nearly forty years, Babs was my other half. I bounced every idea off her and she off me. We thought, we decided, we navigated by sonar. Without her, the mechanism is broken. I don't know where I am or where I'm going — a submarine dead in the water, a whale without a mate.

Two, four, six, eight, how shall we now cogitate?

Descartes was right. I can't think so I don't exist. I died the day she died. This is a dream like in that story by Ambrose Bierce where the hanged man dreams his miraculous escape.

I'll count to ten and pinch myself and wake up wherever the dead go, if the dead go.

It's the ping that's missing. A computer on a network sends out tiny signals. *Ping. Ping.* I'm here. Are you there? Please send a ping back so I know where you are, that you are, so I know where I am and that I am.

Babs and I used to ping one another hundreds, thousands of times a day—a look, a touch, a word. There didn't need to be any other message. The simple ping that she was there, that she cared, that she was real and I was real, that we sent joy and received joy from one another's presence and existence. The ping pong of life.

Life is action and reaction, actor and witness. There's no point in falling in the forest if there's no one to hear. Witnesses for one another, confirming one another's reality, that we are not alone, that we are one another's best friend, partner, mate. I'm okay, you're okay. I love you and you love me. Without those signals sensed and six-sensed, I'm lost. And general sociability can't undo that. Crowds are lonely. The noise and bustle of strangers provide no nourishment.

A ping, a true ping is intimate. You feel it and you send it with the depths of your being.

I half expected the pings to continue beyond the grave. But they didn't. She was gone. So I was gone. The I-Thou that had been us, the couple who had been us no longer existed. And I didn't know who I was anymore.

I want to reinvent the wheel of life and love. I want to reach out across the dining room table and take the hand of this intriguing, attractive purple-haired lady and find out if sparks fly between our fingertips.

Nonsense. Total nonsense. There's no such thing as magic, thought Abe.

And despite himself, he thought and prayed, "Please, lady, please prove me wrong."

5 ~ Gentleman Johnny Burgoyne

As soon as he finished eating, Abe left abruptly, telling Mercy that he had "things to do," that he had to "unpack and everything". But he had nothing to do at all.

He went exploring, wandering through the long twisting hallways and the above-ground tunnels that connected the dozen buildings as a single complex. The half dozen TV rooms were all crowded. The library was empty. In the card room, he spotted a bridge game and half a dozen people playing solitaire.

In the distance, he spotted Mercy walking arm-in-arm with a short bald round man who looked like Gimli, the ax-wielding dwarf from the *Lord of the Rings* movies, only without the beard. Maybe that was her brother, Jemmie.

At first Abe wasn't sure if it was Mercy. Then their eyes met, and she turned abruptly, guiding her brother in the opposite direction.

He had offended her. He had blown it. He wasn't surprised, but he was disappointed. Part of him had hoped that she was so attracted to him that she wouldn't be put off by his sudden departure from breakfast.

Abe went to lunch early and sat at the same table. She arrived later with the round little man and she was talking to a tall athletic dark-haired lady. She avoided making eye contact with him and veered off to the other end of the dining room where she sat with her back toward him. She was soon joined by a couple. The man, well over six feet tall, had the posture and presence of someone in authority. His wife, who needed to be slowly guided to the table as if she were blind, had bright blond hair, carefully braided in an elaborate bun. In sharp contrast to the elegance and apparent youth of her hair, the skin of her neck and arms hung loose and wrinkled.

Abe stayed at his table long after he had finished eating, in part because he had nowhere to go and nothing to do, and in part hoping that Mercy would acknowledge him when she walked by him on her way out. But she and her party left by a back door.

He spent the afternoon in the TV room nearest to his apartment. He awoke from a calm and trance-like state when those around him shuffled by, hurrying to dinner. He had no recollection of what he had watched. He was well on his way to becoming a mindless, sedentary old man, no more alive than the Victorian furniture.

He didn't look for Mercy in the dining room, and he paid little attention to the food in the buffet, throwing a bit of this and a bit of that on his plate, without noticing or caring what it was. He hadn't been this depressed since the day after Babs died.

Then Mercy was beside him, and, with a bright smile, she took his arm and guided him to the table where her brother and the tall dark-haired lady and the couple were seated.

"Abe," she announced, "I'd like you to meet my brother, Jemmie, and Cat, a yoga guru and history expert, a great partner for Trivial Pursuit. This here's Dick, a former school superintendent who knows everything about everything; and his wife Belle who mostly lives in a world of her own, but sometimes shows flashes of her old self.

"So, Abe, why don't you introduce yourself? I served you my life story for breakfast, telling you more about me than these, my closest friends know. Now it's your turn to open up. Who are you? What matters to you? What brings you here?"

"I'm retired," Abe began. "I taught English at a private high school. My wife, Babs, died three years ago, when she was 64 and I 67. We were married for 39 years."

"Okay," Mercy coaxed him, "now tell us the whole story—the truth and the whole truth, and not just the Cliff Notes."

"If you insist. But first, tell me please, was what you told me this morning true?" he dared to ask. "What you said about you and your husband both having cancer and your brother being struck by lightning at your husband's funeral? That's too bizarre to be real."

"Every life is bizarre, the result of a chain of improbable occurrences. Only average people lead average lives, and there is no *average person*. Dick taught me that and can say it far better than I. Now get on with your story."

"My wife died suddenly. Not in an instant. In a few hours. But it felt like poof—she was gone. I became a different person because she wasn't there anymore."

"Ouch."

"That eloquent word sums it up well. Before, I was a teacher of English at a co-ed private boarding school. I was retirement age but had no intention of retiring. There was a rhythm to my life, to our lives. Babs taught French at the same school. We were house parents in one of the dorms. Our wages weren't princely; but we had free housing, free food, three months off in the summer and three weeks around Christmas and three weeks in the spring. We used the school-year breaks to connect with our two kids and their families. Los Angeles one break and Georgia the next. We spent our summers in France, Paris or the South, her choice. Wherever she was, was home.

"Off and on, I was writing an autobiographical novel. I was in no hurry. Life was sweet, and I would rather live it than write about it. My job gave me a chance to reread and talk about books that I loved.

"Then, poof—nothing made sense. I couldn't teach. I retired and moved into an apartment. I didn't unpack. Everything was in boxes, stacked floor to ceiling. I lived in front of the TV, ordered groceries and necessities online. I rarely left the apartment.

"It was a challenge to remember to eat. I couldn't sleep at night and had trouble keeping my eyes open by day. I binge-watched old TV series, series I had watched with Babs. I could enter those worlds that she had once enjoyed, and I could imagine her enjoying them again with me.

"It was a year before I could read a newspaper, two years before I could read an entire book.

"When I emerged from my depression, I had no project, no goal, no purpose, but I knew I didn't want to be dependent on my kids. I needed to start fresh, on my own terms, in some place that wasn't haunted with memories of where Babs and I had been and what we had done together. I wanted a place that wasn't connected to my past, where maybe I could build a future, some tolerable and pleasant mode of living, where I could cultivate new habits and new interests and try living again instead of rotting in squalor. It's not a romantic dream, but it's progress, solid progress."

"Congratulations on your progress. But you'll need a new name to start a new life," suggested Mercy.

"Sure. Wave your magic wand," Abe chuckled, dismissively.

"Oh, you of little faith," she intoned like a preacher. "Jemmie has an uncanny ability for assigning names."

"You mean nicknames?"

"Nicknames? Call them that if you like. A true believer would call them true names."

Abe couldn't tell if she was kidding.

"We've had great fun with the names Jemmie has given us. So Jemmie, what do you have to say to our new friend?"

"Ah, Johnny!" Jemmie stood up, reached across the table and shook Abe's hand. "So glad to meet you, sir."

"Excuse me. My name isn't Johnny. I'm Abe."

"Just Abe," added Mercy with a grin.

Jemmie replied to his sister. "No, my dear. This is Gentleman Johnny Burgoyne, General Burgoyne, hero of Saratoga and acclaimed playwright on the London stage."

6 ~ The Name Game

Dick was a commanding presence, born to be a leader, towering a head taller than Abe. Abe had to stretch his head back to look Dick in the eye. And Dick spoke with such authority that you had to look him in the eye. Abe regretted not having followed up on Mercy's comment about average people and asked Dick him how every life could be unique.

"Imagine a kaleidoscope, with trillions of pieces," Dick intoned. "Different colors, sizes, and shapes. Every time the kaleidoscope turns, a different pattern appears. The patterns have similarities. You can, by ignoring variations, define categories so you can talk about what you see. But every pattern is, in fact, one-of-a-kind."

Abe made the mistake of following up, "But what does that have to do with ordinary lives being unique?"

"The chain of events that led to me becoming who I am and the one that led to you becoming who you are were highly unlikely—one coincidence happening after another. If any event in the chain had not unfolded just the way it did, everything would have turned out differently.

"The apparent likelihood of events depends on your perspective when recalling them. You know all the details related to coincidences that have affected the course of your own life. And the more you know about an event, the more unique it seems to you. But those same events, when seen by someone else and considered separately rather than in sequence, are subject to laws of probability and seem ordinary and expected.

"Every time you toss a coin, the probability of heads is 50%, regardless of the results of previous tosses. But a long chain of events—heads, heads, tails, heads, tails—defies analysis.

"It's possible to predict with great accuracy the average outcome of many similar events, but it's impossible to predict, with certainty, any single event. In other words, the more you know about a specific event and the circumstances that led to it, the more unique and miraculous that event appears. Known in detail, all events are highly unlikely, the result of multiple chains of coincidence.

"Think about the events that led to your first falling in love. All the pieces fell into place miraculously, and it's difficult to imagine how your life could have gone if those very unlikely events had not occurred when and how they did. Every moment of every life is unique and miraculous."

"I warned you," said Mercy, who was sitting to on Abe's other side. Abe was relieved to break eye contact with Dick and to turn toward her.

"Another piece of advice," she added with a smile. "Never sit next to Dick."

Abe looked at her in disbelief.

"That's not rude," she insisted. "It's a matter of self-defense. You can't help but pay attention to what he says and looking up at him puts a strain on your neck. So, we leave an empty chair on either side of him."

"You always share the same table?"

"Often, very often. There's a bunch of us who eat together and hang out together. Jemmie calls us the Extraordinary Ladies of Arcadia. Cat and Belle and me, and three others you haven't met yet. Plus a few accompanying gentlemen, Jemmie and Dick and now you. There are far too few gentlemen here. You don't live long enough," she added.

"And Jemmie gives you all names?"

"Not all of us, Johnny," Dick chimed in. "Only a favored few. My wife Belle is just Belle. That's what I've always called her, from 'Michele my Belle' in the song. Jemmie hasn't named her, and she, in the early stages of Alzheimer's, really needs an identity. Even a fake one would be good for her."

"And you, Dick? What does he call you?"

"Sheridan. Richard Brinsley Sheridan, the playwright. Dick works fine for that. And I rather like the association, having written a play back in college. That was my path not followed, but one I could imagine for myself. By the way, that makes us friends, you know—in a parallel world. Burgoyne was a playwright as well as a general. After he was captured at the Battle of Saratoga and was shipped home, he became a playwright, popular on the London stage, a friend of and collaborator with my alter ego, Sheridan."

"How can you believe such nonsense? How can you treat the random choices of Jemmie as if they meant something? Pardon me if I don't have faith in his intuition. General Burgoyne. That's simply absurd. And these other names, Mercy and Jemmie and Cat, do they have links to history as well? Are you all play-acting? Is that how you amuse yourselves here?"

"Jemmie calls himself James Otis, after the Revolutionary leader, and his sister he calls Mercy Otis Warren, the playwright and historian. Cat he calls Catharine Macaulay after the first British woman historian."

Mercy laughed, "We've had great fun trying on the new names, just as I have fun with new wigs. It adds a dimension to who we are and who we can be."

7 ~ Perchance to Dream

Too much too soon, too many people with too many realities, thought Abe as he retreated to the library after dinner. He wanted to be alone, and he wanted to double-check the nonsense he had just heard.

He wasn't sure which of them annoyed him the most—Cat with her memory for historical details or Dick who spoke with such authority about the unknowable.

At least Cat had a rational explanation for the naming. She spoke of parallel lives. These people in a nursing home in the twenty-first century were similar in some way to people from the past, like Plutarch writing biographies in pairs, based on similarities, matching a Greek and a Roman: Theseus and Romulus, Alexander the Great and Julius Caesar. She also thought of the naming like roles assigned by a director who sensed a resonance between who you are and the part you are to play.

Abe had protested, "But why in God's name would Jemmie call me Burgoyne? I'm nothing like Burgoyne. I have nothing in my character that would incline me to act the way he did."

But Cat had insisted, "We all have the seeds of different personalities. Given the right circumstances, we could become different people. You could be Burgoyne. I see the Burgoyne in you."

"But I'm a retired high school teacher. An English teacher at a private school. I haven't a smidgen of military inclination."

"But if you, like the original Burgoyne, had been born in 1722 into a genteel family that had no hereditary wealth, you would have had few career choices. Of course, you could have been apprenticed into a trade, but that would have meant a permanent drop in social status. Your real choices were the church or the military."

"Certainly not the church."

"And you would have made the best of your military career. And if you went to a private school like the one where you taught in this life time, and if your best friend at that school had a witty pretty sister who took a shine to you and you to her, and her father told you to back off and never have anything to do with her, what would you have done?"

Richard Seltzer

"To hell with the old man. If she and I wanted, we would elope."

"And so, you did. And the old man, the Earl of Derby, cut his daughter off without a penny and wanted nothing more to do with either of you."

"And what's the meaning of all of this?"

"I'm saying that if you had been born into the same circumstances, in the same time and place that Burgoyne was, you might have followed a life path very much like the one that he did."

In the library, Abe found the Encyclopedia Britannica. By chance it was the eleventh edition from 1910, the very best edition, the one that was the starting point for Wikipedia. He read the article on Burgoyne. Then he found a book-length biography of Burgoyne and skimmed that. And, yes, incredibly, Cat had her facts right, though she hadn't mentioned that Burgoyne gambled recklessly and that he had several children with his mistress, an actress and opera singer.

Cat's present-day back-story had surprised him. She said that when she was nearly fifty, a tenured professor of political science and history, she married a recent college grad and a former student. It was scandalous. She was more than twice his age. What a mismatch. Everyone presumed that she would die long before him. But as it turned out, they only had ten years together before he was killed in a car crash. When she retired, she morphed into a yoga guru. Now in her mid-seventies, tall, thin, and muscular, a Jane Fonda look-alike, she could have passed for twenty years younger. Her alter ego, Catharine Macaulay, had also scandalously married a much younger man. That and the fascination with history may have been why she so readily accepted the name that Jemmie had chosen for her.

As for Dick, his height, his bulk, his physical presence were enough to aggravate Abe. At five foot ten, Abe had never considered himself as short, but Dick was nearly a foot taller than him. Abe was now five nine, an inch shorter than he was ten years before. He wasn't expecting that— not bent over, standing straight and tall. He knew that it was the cartilage in his spine wearing down or shrinking, but how much more would he shrink? Should he start making marks on the wall like he did as a kid when he was recording how much he grew? Depressing.

From their interaction at the dinner table, Abe knew that Mercy looked up to Dick, both literally and figuratively. In his presence, she had a look of admiration, almost worship. If Belle weren't around, she'd want to connect with Dick, and he with her. And Belle wasn't likely to be around much longer.

Dick had explained that Belle had Alzheimer's. The police found her at three in the morning, in December, walking down the middle of Main Street in Sturbridge, Massachusetts, in her nightgown, carrying a suitcase stuffed with clothes, and looking for a taxi to take her to Philadelphia. At that point, she knew her name. She even knew her address. She was lucky the police found her before she was hit by a car or died of exposure. But it was clearly Alzheimer's. The doctor connected Dick with a support group for caregivers of Alzheimer's victims. Her condition was irreversible. It would steadily get worse. Sooner or later, she'd need to be institutionalized with 24/7 care. The doctor recommended that he find an assisted-living facility with attached nursing home and Alzheimer's wing. Then there would be a guarantee that she'd go to the top of the waiting list when the time came. She would get the next available slot as soon as someone died. Otherwise, it might be years before he could get her into an Alzheimer's facility since the demand was great. Yes, years of hell, caring for someone who had no idea who he was or even who she was. They moved here two years ago. Dick was surprised that Belle had been able to stay in assisted-living this long.

It was naive to presume that Mercy was unattached, available. She was in Dick's on-deck circle, and Dick knew it.

She had reminded Abe that she was going to deliver a special sermon in the morning and that she expected him to attend. But she had reminded everyone else, too. Yes, she was warm toward him, but with the warmth of friendship, welcoming him as a new member of her social group.

Abe could barely remember the others who joined them later at the dinner table. They went by their Jemmie-assigned names: Aphra, Nell, and Fanny. More of the Extraordinary Ladies of Arcadia. Abe had told Mercy that she reminded him of Meg Ryan. Then she compared Cat to Jane Fonda and paired Aphra to Bette Midler, Nell to Scarlett Johansson, and Fannie to Keira Knightley. Flattering comparisons. More like the mothers or grandmothers of those actresses. But helpful mnemonics for him. And another kind of parallel lives.

Abe fell asleep in a La-Z-Boy reclining chair in the library and dreamt that he needed to go to South Korea and back, immediately. That's what he told Babs, and she believed him without question. He went to the local airport, which looked like a bus station, and said he needed a ticket to South Korea. The lady at the counter looked at him like he was crazy and didn't say a word. Finally, he asked, "You mean I have to go by way of Kennedy?"

"Yes."

He took out his cellphone and was about to open the Uber app. Then he realized this didn't make sense. It would cost far too much and take far too long to go to Seoul and back. He phoned Babs to tell her. She answered, "Yes?" But he didn't say a thing to her. Seoul. Yes, Soul. He realized that Babs was dead.

He was walking down Commonwealth Avenue, heading toward the Boston Common at night. He stopped short, staring at a double shadow. Then he walked again and saw a double shadow form again. Walking between lamp posts, as he approached the half-way point, the shadow from the one light crossed the shadow from the next.

Memory dreams flashed in quick succession. He saw Babs in her college dorm room as she was when he first met her. He was dating her roommate, and Babs threw a wet washcloth at him. He saw the two of them holding hands on their first date at the movie *King of Hearts*. Their wedding. The births of their two kids. Her sudden stomach pains the night before she died. Everyone gathered at her graveside for the funeral.

Suddenly, it was Halloween and he was ten, going trick-or-treat door-to-door. He was dressed like a Revolutionary general. The girl beside him was a witch with purple hair.

Then, Abe was about to be sent away to boarding school—the Westminster School in London, beside Westminster Abbey. He was about to begin a new life, going to a prestigious school where he would make friends with the children of important people who would one day be important themselves. This was a rite of passage. He would no longer be a child. He'd be a little man, a man in the making. That meant he had to give up childish things, including his friends: the neighbor kids he had known for as long as he could remember. These were country kids, children of tradesmen and craftsmen, equals in the world of children, but inferiors in the world of men. He would miss Jack and Tom, and Mary, too, who was as fast of foot and as quick of wit as any boy. Mary, who sometimes looked at him in a way that made him forget the world of men and ambition, to make him think that all he wanted was to lie by her side with her hand in his, her head on his shoulder, connected, together, forever and ever.

She could read as well as any boy. He had helped her with that, since her folks couldn't afford a tutor, and didn't believe that girls needed book-learning. She had read all his books and dozens more that he had gotten for her from his father's library. She liked to write stories. They would spin tales together and then she'd write them down, adding pages to the makeshift book they were building and that they kept hidden under a loose board in the attic.

Mary was sewing now with her mother—one of her many chores. This was his last day before he had to leave, and she was sewing. He wanted her here and now in the attic. He lifted the loose boards where they hid the book she was writing. He spread a quilt and lay down on it as the two of them had done last week. Mary's mother was at market, so Mary was free for a few hours. They were bundling, lying side by side with a wooden support separating them. They pretended they were teenagers who were courting, and they cheated a smidgen, getting closer than they were supposed to. He stretched to put his shoulder on top of the support, and she stretched to put her head on his shoulder. They planned to elope and stow away on a ship to America and start a new life in a land where all men were equal, and all women were equal with them, and they could make whatever future they wanted together.

He woke up. He was a seventy-year-old man who had drifted off to sleep in the library of an old folks' home.

He went his apartment and went to bed. Then totally unlike himself, he slept through the night and woke up too late for breakfast, but early enough for Mercy's sermon.

***

How sweet, thought Mercy when she went to bed that night. I've known this man for less than a day. We haven't so much as held hands. And he acts jealous when I pay attention to another man. How flattering. I feel like I'm in high school. Who would ever expect romance in an assisted living facility?

Maybe I should wear my red wig in the morning. No. It's Lent. I'll stick with the purple for church services.

And what would life be like with him, if it turns out that we connect? Who might I become? Who might he become?

And the name "Johnny." I'll tease him with Johnny. It's delightful how he overreacts to that name—as if it makes a difference, as if it reflects on who he really is. He doth protest too much.

***

Mercy couldn't remember the details of her dream that night. She rarely remembered dreams. But she knew that it had to do with bundling, probably prompted by a section of the mural in the dining room that she had noticed for the first time at dinner last night. A love and marriage section with bundling as one of the steps. At the end of the series the young couple were sitting in a carriage and presumably singing the song about love and marriage from the movie *Friendly Persuasion*. The dream was probably prompted, too, by her memories of her childhood summer jobs at Plimouth Plantation, reenacting colonial life and sometimes demonstrating bundling for the tourists with her neighbor Jake. She wondered if Dick might have done that as well, growing up in Sturbridge, and working summers at Sturbridge Village.

Bundling, she thought, what a sweet romantic idea. A young, married couple spending a whole night together, unsupervised, fully clothed but lying side-by-side, cuddling, holding hands, and talking about anything and everything all night long, just enjoying being together. What an excellent tradition. If young people today did that, they'd probably make fewer mistakes in picking a mate.

8 ~ A Tale of Two Pianos

Bright daylight flooded the activity room. The ceiling was thirty feet high, with wooden struts and supports. There were a dozen large windows—great for light, but too high to look out and enjoy the view. A wooden ladder led to a square-shaped cupola on of the roof above.

This room had originally been the loft of a barn, attached to a house. In its reincarnation as part of a girls' school, it was the auditorium and basketball court, with a stage equipped for performing plays. The basketball backstops were still in place, as was the stage. There was a vintage upright piano in the front of the room, and another piano in the back. Folding chairs were lined up for the anticipated audience.

When Abe arrived, Mercy was sitting at the piano at the front of the room. She looked very small in the vastness of the empty space around her, but she also looked self-directed, determined, very much in charge, as she opened and organized hymnals and sheet music until she was satisfied that everything was lined up the way she wanted it. Only then did she acknowledge Abe's presence, "Ah, Johnny. Glad you could make it despite your busy schedule."

"Yes," he joked. "it was difficult to fit you in, but nothing could be more important than your sermon."

"I'm glad you appreciate the importance of my words," she countered. "And how does your new name feel? Getting used to a new name is like getting used to a new pair of shoes. At first it may feel tight and unnatural, but you'll get used to it."

Before Abe had a chance to protest her name nonsense, Jemmie came barreling into the room, running stiff-legged.

"What's the matter with Jemmie?" Abe asked.

"Nothing. That's just Jemmie being Jemmie. He sees the cupola as the crow's nest of a pirate ship, and he acts like Long John Silver with a peg-leg."

Jemmie climbed the ladder, haltingly, stiff-legged, then gestured dramatically from his perch and proclaimed, "Avast ye bland blubbers. All fingers on deck. Burn blubber. Shuffle the deck. Man the goons.

Spanish galleon off the port bow-wow. Any port in a storm. Any storm in a cloud."

"Enough, Jemmie. Come on down. I want Johnny to see the view. This is new to him."

Jemmie obeyed without objection. Then Mercy took Abe's hand and led him to the ladder. He enjoyed glimpses of her shapely legs that appeared under her ankle-length black skirt as she ascended above him.

In the cupola, Mercy stood facing the window, looking toward the Old Man of the Mountains. Abe stood close behind her, striving to avoid inappropriate contact in the tight space, and looking over her right shoulder.

The roof was covered with two feet of freshly fallen snow, marked here and there with footprints of birds or elves.

Mercy said, "It looks like the Old Man is wearing a white hat."

A flock of geese flew in formation first one way, then another, then another.

"Have they lost their sense of time?" asked Abe. "Are they migrating in mid-winter?"

"No. Remember the clock, the broken clock. The story is in the brochure that you must have read. Legend has it that this is the place where time stopped. The geese agree. No matter what the season, they stay put. They fly around for the joy of flying, but they don't go anywhere. They'll land by the kitchen door at lunchtime, and the staff will feed them scraps, as they always do."

Abe was reminded of the cupola on the house where he grew up in Plymouth, New Hampshire. It was a favorite destination in the game of sardines at his birthday party in the seventh grade. The tightness of the space was its main attraction, being forced into close contact with a girl he would have been too shy to talk to, much less hold. And when a girl hid there, that was a sign she wanted contact. A few years later he would climb up there with his hand-holding girlfriend, Madeline. She, standing in front of him, her back toward him, and he leaning into her and holding her tight. Only this wasn't Madeline, it was Mercy, and she suddenly turned, gave him a peck on the lips, and she flashed a smile. He was truly in *Arcadia* on the first morning of the rest of his life.

Parallel Lives

He put his arms around her, hoping for more. But she tapped his forehead with her index finger—a gentle reproof. "Enough. More than enough. It's time to sing some *hims* and some hers, and for me to explain the nature of the universe to the assembled congregation."

She smiled, gave him a hug, rested her head on his right shoulder, then stepped down the ladder.

As the audience settled in their seats, Mercy sat at the piano in the front of the room and played hymns. Abe sat in the back row on the far left. The ladies of Arcadia sat together in the front row.

The piano was at an angle, so Abe could see Mercy in profile. And because she was fully occupied and was the natural focus of attention, Abe had the leisure to stare at her, without being rude. Yes, Meg Ryan: the light blue eyes, the small mouth with cupid's bow upper lip, the short, straight, delicate nose, high cheek bones and pointy chin. The impression she gave was that she was always one step ahead and thinking the next thought while speaking the present one. She was alert, aware, quick to judge, quick to forgive, and quick to kiss. She was confident and self-assertive.

Mercy played and sang one hymn after another: Amazing Grace, Holy Holy Holy, A Mighty Fortress is Our God, All Things Bright and Beautiful, The Old Rugged Cross, Rock of Ages, and more. Then walking to the podium, she sang, "Purple is the color of my true love's hair, in the morning ..."

"Yes, purple is the color of Lent," she began. "I'm liturgically correct this morning. Please forgive me for that. That's even worse than being politically correct. But I felt like purple this morning, and I wasn't going to wear a different color just to be incorrect.

"Today, I want to talk about the magic we don't notice because it doesn't make sense, and what doesn't make sense can't be real.

"In the Enlightenment, wit was defined as the ability to see similarities and connections; and judgment was the ability to see differences. Wit was seen as a dangerous talent. You could be too clever. Sober judgment and reason needed to keep the upper hand.

"We ignore much of what we perceive because we judge and censor it. If it doesn't fit in the version of the world that we are used to and on which we base our everyday actions, our web of understanding, our

37

notion of how everything fits together, we ignore it. Because if we admit the reality of something that doesn't fit, the structure falls apart.

"The task of reason is not to understand the world, but rather to deal with it. Reason blocks out or modifies what we perceive so that we can be confident that everything conforms to the standard model of what we expect.

"When we sleep, reason rests and in our dreams the perceptions that reason edited out have full rein and the impossible happens.

"Some drugs can have a similar effect, turning off the blinders and constraints of reason and allowing us to become conscious of the perceptions that reason would deny.

"When learning to draw, we have to train ourselves to see things the way they are rather than the way we have learned to think they are, breaking our habits of thinking, restoring the abilities we had as children, before reason began to dominate perception. We need to learn to see not just what we are focusing on, but the periphery. It's like a character in a legend who notices a leprechaun or a fairy out of the corner of her eye, and it vanishes when she tries to look at it directly.

"It's a left-brain right-brain thing: the left side of the brain being the seat of reason, and the right side the seat of intuition and emotion. There are exercises we can do to reduce the strength of left-side control and to learn to see without censorship, to open ourselves up to new perceptions.

"You all know my brother Jemmie. He looks at the world differently. Sometimes he retreats to his own world. Then, when he comes back, he blesses us with what he found there. If he had been born at another time, in another culture, he might have become a shaman or a holy wandering pilgrim or a court jester.

"He was struck by lightning a few years ago. He survived, but with damage to the left side of his brain. Sometimes he seems to babble nonsense. Other times his words provoke us to look at ourselves or others in a different way.

"Reality is messy. Pay attention to the unintended as well as the intended. To enjoy the story of your life, suspend your disbelief.

"Remember the old days when cameras were mechanical and used film and there were many ways to make mistakes. Remember double exposures? I wish I could get that effect with the camera in my cellphone. Sometimes I don't want a perfect picture, I don't want the photo to show exactly what I saw. Sometimes I'd like to see what it would look like out of focus or with multiple exposures, to bring out some aspect of the scene that went unnoticed before. I want the camera to help me to unsee, to unremember, to look afresh.

"Think of sound and music, the sound behind and within what we call music. With mechanical instruments, as opposed to electronic ones, there's always background noise and unintended sounds generated by the instruments. We have trained our ears to hear only the music, the primary sounds, and to filter out the noise. Try to imagine the experience of paying attention to all the sounds, not just the ones that our reason selects as music. Maybe perfect pitch is a defect, rather than a gift, censoring extraneous noises, and the person with a tin ear hears everything.

"Dick, I'd like you to help me with a demonstration. There are two pianos here in our activity room. We always use the upright in the front here. But there is also a player piano in the back. It used to serve as a surface for putting a TV on, before the coming of flat screens. Now it's just a catchall for pictures. It would probably have been thrown away long ago, but it would cost too much to haul it away, and it would be an eyesore if they dumped it outside. But it still works. When the roll for a song turns, the keys go up and down, generating music as if a ghost were playing. A vacuum is built up by bellows that are driven by electric power. A paper roll is pulled over a metal bar with a row of punch holes, one hole for each tone. I've loaded the roll for 'Amazing Grace.' Turn it on, Dick."

The player piano did its thing, and Mercy joined in, playing along on the upright. First both pianos sounded the same. Then Mercy deliberately played out of sync, a fraction of a second before and then a fraction behind the player piano like one was an echo of the other, and they switched which was real and which the echo.

"Imagine what it would it be like to stand on a cliff and hear the words you mean to say a moment before you say them?

"I enjoy playing duets like this, creating a musical shadow—now in front and now behind, giving a sense of depth, of three-dimensionality.

If you listen carefully to traditional pianos, rather than electronic ones, each piano has its peculiarities, not just that this key or that one is out of tune, but the unintended mechanical noises and after-effects that vary depending on how you strike the keys.

"Johnny, I want you to shut your eyes, stand up, and turn around a dozen times until you feel dizzy and don't know where the front of the room is and where the back. Don't do it yet. Wait for my signal. Then I want you to listen to a piece of music and identify it. Turn now."

Answering to the name Johnny without hesitation, Abe obediently turned a dozen times. Then hearing the music, he said, "That's Bach's Goldberg Variations."

"Well done. And did you hear that on the player piano or was that me at the upright?"

"I guess it was the player piano."

"Thank you, Johnny. You can open your eyes and sit down now. That was me, playing honky-tonk style, a style that emphasizes rhythm more than melody or harmony—a style developed in the days when many pianos were poorly cared for, out of tune, and often had some non-functioning keys. It's a style in which the mechanical noises of the instrument where part of the experience. I find it refreshing sometimes to play that way on an old piano and savor the noise as well as the music, to feel the music playing hide-and-seek with the noise. It's a way to train my ear, like drawing helps train my eye. It's a way to notice what my mind would otherwise edit out."

She smiled, having successfully delivered an entertaining sermon. Then music came from the back of the room. Jemmie was sitting at the player piano and moving his hands over the keys as it played Bach's Goldberg Variations, honky-tonk style.

The audience applauded so he played it again and again.

Mercy stared in amazement, then explained her dismay. "There's no roll for that tune. Jemmie is playing that himself. But he doesn't know how to play the piano. He never had lessons."

Then Jemmie played and sang, "Carry me Bach, to old Virginie." And everyone joined in.

Mercy laughed. "This didn't happen because we know it can't happen."

9 ~ Can You See?

"Good God! You looked like you meant that," Abe told Mercy after everyone but their group had left the activity room. "You really don't know how Jemmie did that, do you?"

"I don't know," she admitted. "But I'm getting used to strange things happening here."

"Are you kidding me? As if this place is haunted?"

"No. Not haunted. I think it's more a matter of perception, like in my sermon. We see more. We notice more. There's magic in everyday life in the everyday world, but we don't notice it, or we don't think of it that way. Birth and death and growing old; life itself, we don't understand what it is or where it comes from or how and why it ends. Maybe there are cracks in the fabric of reality here. Or maybe such things happen and go unnoticed elsewhere; but here we're more sensitive and we're more willing to believe what we see and hear. Finding sand in my shoes. Jemmie knowing how to play the piano. His naming—whatever his naming means. When such things happen here, we're alert to them. Not for what they are in and of themselves, but as clues that could lead us, that are supposed to lead us to some sort of revelation."

Abe laughed dismissively. "Pilgrim's Progress."

"What?"

"I'm reminded of allegories where events in everyday life have a second meaning—a parallel story. You don't believe that kind of nonsense, do you?"

"I don't know what to believe. But I do know that there's much I don't understand."

"And you think that there's something weird and unworldly about what goes on here?"

"No. I don't think this place is any weirder than another. But maybe our senses are heightened here because of the special circumstances that drew us here. Here the distractions of everyday life have been removed. The world is no longer too much with us. It's like sensory deprivation therapy. We see and feel more intensively because there's so little to see and feel. Our attention is focused like never before. It's a matter of what we can see."

Jemmie started playing the Star-Spangled Banner and singing "Oh say can you see?"

Abe stared at Jemmie and said, "That's uncanny."

"Yes. Indeed," added Cat.

Abe was embarrassed to realize that Cat was standing next to him, paying attention to what he said. He had presumed that Mercy and he were having a private conversation, and that the others were involved in talk of their own. Cat was a couple of inches taller than Abe, and Mercy was a couple of inches shorter. Abe had to tilt his head to shift his attention from the one to the other.

Mercy continued, "I have no idea how Jemmie can play like that, or how he comes up with the names, how he could know as much as he does about history. He never studied history. He never showed any interest in it. Cat's the one who has been most aware of the strangeness of the names he has given us and the history behind them. I've been dismissive of her facts and theories before, but maybe now I should suspend my disbelief."

Cat joined in, "So now you're ready to take me seriously? You're willing to admit that Jemmie's knowledge of history and his coming up with these names is out of the ordinary?"

"What do you mean?" asked Abe.

"Well, take my name. He calls me Catharine Macaulay. She was the first woman historian in Britain. She lived in the eighteenth century and wrote about the seventeenth. She was a good friend of Mercy Warren, even though they lived on opposite sides of the Atlantic. They corresponded, and Catharine made a long visit to the newly independent United States. Like me, Catharine married a man less than half her age, scandalizing her contemporaries. She was a staunch republican, uncompromising, sticking by her principles, regardless of the social, political, and financial consequences. They called her a 'virago.'"

"Do you mean Virgo?" asked Mercy. "That's my sign and I'm proud of it. That means intelligence, attention to detail, common sense, and commitment."

"No. Virago. That's the same as a harridan."

"What's a harridan?" Mercy asked Abe, as if expecting him, as an English teacher, to know.

He was relieved that Cat answered before he could admit his ignorance.

"A termagant."

"And what's a termagant?"

"A vixen."

"You mean like one of Rudolph's reindeer friends?"

"No. I mean a shrew."

"As in Shakespeare?" asked Mercy. "A nasty ill-tempered woman who needs to be tamed? Well, she must have had plenty of company back in her day for them to need all those words: virago, harridan, termagant, vixen, and shrew. There must have been a lot of women who weren't about to sit quietly with their knitting and let men run their lives, women who would stand up to men and make men regret it if they didn't get out of their way."

"And me, Cat, what about me?" asked the lady who could have been Scarlett Johansson's mother or even her grandmother. Green eyes and red hair. Her hair looked natural, not bright and artificial like Mercy's wigs. It looked restored to what might have been its original shade, by persistent and expensive care, with no sign of gray roots. "He calls me Nell. That has a sweet sound to it, but what might he mean by that?"

"Nell Gwyn, I believe. An actress, more than three hundred years ago."

"I didn't know they had actresses back then. Wasn't it illegal for women to perform on the stage in Shakespeare's day? Didn't men have to play the women's parts?"

"This was after that. Cromwell and the Puritans executed the king and outlawed theater as immoral. More than a hundred years later, in the days of Mercy Warren, theater was still illegal in Massachusetts. None of her plays were ever performed during her lifetime."

"So how did Nell, my Nell, end up an actress?"

"The Restoration. The kings came back. Charles II, the son of the king who lost his head, became king, and morality was turned upside down. He opened the theaters, let women perform on stage, and made Nell, the most famous actress of the day, his favorite mistress."

"He had others?"

"Half a dozen, I believe. I-I mean my other self, Catharine Macaulay, wrote about it."

"And Fanny?" asked the lady who looked like the mother or grandmother of Keira Knightley. Abe could imagine her fighting side-by side with her grandchildren in Pirates of the Caribbean movies. "What can you say about me? Not Fanny Hill, I hope."

"Fanny Burney and Madame d'Arblay."

"Which one?"

"They are one and the same. Fanny Burney was a novelist, a generation before Jane Austen. As a young girl, her father favored her two older, brilliant and beautiful sisters. He sent them off to Paris for their education, but Fanny, the runt of the litter, had to fend for herself at home. By the age of eight, she still didn't know the alphabet; but by ten she was writing stories. Self-taught, she became one of the most popular novelists of her day. She became the 'Keeper of the Robes' for Queen Charlotte, the wife of King George III. Then at forty-one, an old maid by the standards of the day, she got married, for the first time, to an exiled French nobleman. That's how she became 'Madame d'Arblay,' and under that name she wrote one of the most famous diaries of all time."

"And Aphra? What the hell is an Aphra? A hair style? An aphrodisiac?" asked the woman who looked like she could be Bette Midler's mother—full figured and proud of it. Ready to hug you with one hand and slap you with the other.

"I'm stumped on that one," admitted Cat. "Do you have any idea, Dick?"

"Beats me," he admitted. "Does anybody have a contraband cell phone? We could look it up on Wikipedia,"

"For shame," objected Mercy. "Thinkest thou that any of us would break the God-given commandments we live by."

"Verily, my lady," Dick replied. "Thou speakest true. Prithee forgive my unworthy thought."

"So now we thee-and-thou?" asked Abe.

"How now, brown thou," quipped Jemmie.

"We're going to have to do some research," suggested Dick.

"Get to thee to a lie-brary and lie me some lies," added Jemmie.

10 ~ The Lie-brary

Leaving the dining room and heading for the library, Dick ordered tea and cookies for eight as they passed the front desk. That was one of the perks of assisted living at Arcadia Estates.

The walls had bookcases from floor to ceiling. There was an excellent collection of seventeenth and eighteenth century American and British history and fiction. Many of the volumes dated back to the original owner who was reputed to be a friend of Hawthorne, with many books about Puritans and witchcraft, the Interregnum under Cromwell, the Restoration, colonial America, and the American Revolution. The books were shelved by country, mostly Great Britain and America, and then by date. Most of the books hadn't been touched, except for dusting, in over a hundred years.

Cat quickly found the answer to Aphra's question, "Aphra Behn was a playwright in the seventeenth century and the first woman to make a living as a writer. And here's an article about James Otis, an instigator of the American Revolution. I read about him back in college. Keep in mind that the leaders of the Revolution, the signers of the Declaration, the generals, the Founding Fathers were remarkably lucky. They lost property, but they survived the Revolution unscathed."

"But what about Joseph Warren?" asked Mercy.

"Joseph was killed at the Battle of Bunker Hill. That's a counter example."

"And Nathan Hale?"

"Okay. A young man executed for treason. It's remarkable that there weren't many more like him. You also could mention the nameless soldiers suffering and dying at Valley Forge and the five nameless citizens who died in the Boston Massacre. Tragic, yes, but my point is that they were nameless. None of the men who we know as 'Founding Fathers' was killed in the Revolution. Yes, they were in jeopardy, but they lucked out. Many risked martyrdom, but few paid the price. James Otis was one of the few."

"I never heard of him, except for Jemmie's ramblings. Did he die for the rebel cause?"

"No. Worse. He got his brains bashed and never recovered."

"Well, he wasn't hit by lightning," Abe chuckled. "That would be too much of a coincidence."

"But he was," Cat noted. "Later. More than a decade later. Standing in an open doorway during a thunderstorm. That's what killed him."

"Coincidence," Abe insisted.

"Of course. But he played an important role leading up to the Revolution. It says here that in 1769, at the entrance to the British Coffee House in Boston, James Otis encountered John Robinson, a member of the American Board of Customs Commissioners who was upset about Otis's speeches and newspaper articles attacking the Stamp Act. They fought and Robinson bashed Otis on the head repeatedly with a heavy cane. That was seven years before the Declaration of Independence.

"Remember the discontent that led to the Revolution? The changes in taxation, as Parliament tried to raise revenue and assert tighter control over the colonies? Remember the Stamp Act, the Boston Massacre, the Tea Party? James Otis got that started. His rhetoric and passion changed men's minds and turned loyal British citizens into revolutionaries. He translated the daily news into messages that inflamed the people. 'No taxation without representation,' that was him. He found the guiding principles and natural laws underlying everyday events and hammered his messages home. He was an instigator, a firebrand. Without him those British provocations might have passed with little notice.

"James Otis lit the fire. Others fanned it and added fuel, but he was there at the very start, shouting from the rooftops when few others dared to do so. He was the face of the Revolution long before there was a revolution. And he got his brains bashed for it. He was never the same after that. He'd have moments of clarity, but mostly he was in his own world, mumbling nonsense, not right in his head."

"And this James Otis had a sister named Mercy?" asked Abe.

"Yes. She was a playwright and an historian, the first woman historian in America. She was a friend of John and Abigail Adams. She started the Committees of Correspondence that drew the colonies together on the brink of the Revolution. Her husband was the president of the Massachusetts Provincial Congress and paymaster to Washington's army. Imagine when she heard that General Warren was killed at the Battle of Bunker Hill. Her husband, James Warren, the love of her life, was at that battle, and some called him 'general' in those early disordered times. As it turned out, it was Joseph Warren, not James who died that day. Same last name, but not related, or at least not closely. She felt the risk then and throughout the war."

"And you think that Jemmie knows all this?" asked Abe. "That he's some sort of idiot savant, with encyclopedic knowledge of American history? And what about Burgoyne? Why did he name me Burgoyne? And Sheridan? Why did he name Dick—Sheridan? What's the connection?"

"Give me a minute. It's hard for me to read and talk at the same time."

While Cat read one encyclopedia article after another, Abe found a biography of Burgoyne. Mercy found a volume of Mercy Warren's plays. Aphra found a collection of Aphra Behn's plays, and Nell found a biography of the actress Nell Gwyn.

"Okay," Cat explained. "I think I see the Mercy-Burgoyne connection. Soon after the Battle of Bunker Hill, British troops occupied Boston and were blockaded there by the rebels. This was before the Back Bay was filled in, when it was swampland and part of the harbor, and a narrow peninsula connected the city with the mainland. Boston was easy to blockade. Burgoyne, who was one of the British generals, got bored so he wrote a play and had his soldiers perform it. It was called *The Blockade of Boston*. The one time it was performed, at Faneuil Hall, a soldier ran in screaming 'The rebels are coming.' The crowd erupted in applause at such a brilliant theatrical effect. Only the rebels really were coming. The performance ended, and so did the attack. Burgoyne returned to England soon after that. But Mercy, who had a satirical bent, wrote a play in reply, entitled *The Blockheads*. Her name for England was 'Blunderland.' Mercy and Burgoyne belonged together. Maybe not in that time and place. Maybe on another plane."

"From another airport," Abe mocked her.

"Right," she took his remark in stride. "It took about six weeks to cross the Atlantic in those days, when the weather was good. But suspend your disbelief for a minute. Let's think about Burgoyne. You could make a case that he did more for American independence than anyone else—more than Washington. He was the Father of His Enemy's Country. No one else in his position would have advanced into the wilderness of northern New York with a rag-tag army including wild Indians and German mercenaries who didn't speak English. Anyone else would have insisted on having clear confirmation that General Howe was advancing northward from New York City with a powerful army to join forces with him.

"That was Burgoyne's plan. He knew it would work. He knew it was brilliant. It never occurred to him that Lord Germain, the Secretary of State for America, might forget to send the orders to General Howe. Burgoyne never confirmed that Howe had received the orders, and hence he fell into a trap. His elaborate plan that should have crushed the rebellion and ended the war, wound up giving the rebels a resounding victory at Saratoga, enabling them to win alliances with France and Holland and thereby win the war. Burgoyne and his entire army were captured. He was sent home to England on parole, having given his word of honor that he wouldn't fight the Americans again. And, on his return, he became a friend of Edmund Burke in Parliament, championing the cause of the American colonies. Maybe he wanted the colonists to win in the first place. Maybe that slip-up of his was an unconscious wish.

"In any case, in addition to his political activities, he became a playwright, one of the most popular on the London stage, a friend and competitor of Sheridan. So, there was Mercy in the provincial backwater of Plymouth, Massachusetts, writing plays that could never be performed in Puritan Massachusetts, and there was Burgoyne, a rock star of the London stage. They had a natural affinity, despite the distance between them."

"And how does that affect the price of tea in China?" asked Abe. "Why in God's name would Jemmie call me Burgoyne? And why did he give names to us few, just us?"

"Maybe there will be more," countered Cat. "Maybe this is just the beginning."

"The beginning of what?" asked Abe.

"Maybe that's what we're supposed to find out."

11 ~ Belle

They continued the conversation in the dining room over lunch.

"What about Belle?" Dick asked Cat. "For the rest of us, the name thing is a game, a puzzle, an invitation to play-act. But Belle, with her Alzheimer's really needs an identity, any identity at all. Jemmie, who is she? Do your magic. Tell us who she is or was or could be."

As if a switch had flipped in his brain, Jemmie rattled off, "The bells, bells, bells, bells, bells. The banging and clanging of the bells, and the rebells, and the rebels, and the rebelution."

Belle who had been staring off into space, taking no notice of the conversation around her, sat up straight. "What was that, sir?" she asked while pulling a cosmetics mirror from her pocketbook. Then as she stared at her own face, her jaw dropped, her eyes bulged, and she started shaking wildly.

Dick jumped up, stood behind her chair, and hugged her tight to calm her. But she broke away from him, and kicked him, and swung at him, scratching his face with her fingernails.

She spit in his bloody face. "Stay away from me, you rapist!"

She reached for her steak knife.

He grabbed her wrist.

She kicked him in the groin.

"Honey, it'll be okay," he said softly but firmly. "Let's go back to the apartment. You can lie down and rest. I'll get you some ice cream and cake. You'll feel better. You'll be yourself again."

"Mister, whoever you are, there's no way I'm going to let you in my apartment, much less my bed. I'm not that kind of woman. I don't sleep with strangers. Unhand me, and back off, or I'll scream like you've never heard screaming, and I'll call the police, and I'll tell your mother on you. You've been naughty, very naughty."

A lady in a nurse's uniform stepped between them. Her name tag read "Melody".

"Let me help you, Mrs. Thor."

Before Belle had a chance to reply, Melody had grabbed her arm and given her a shot with a needle.

"A sedative," she explained to Dick. Then, with the help of an orderly, she lowered Belle into a wheelchair.

"I don't want her sedated," Dick protested.

"We're dealing with the necessity of the moment. We don't want her hurting herself or someone else. As it turns out, you're lucky."

"You call this lucky?"

"Mrs. Schneider died this morning. I was about to call the next family on the waiting list. But, if you wish, the spot could be Mrs. Thor's. That's the guarantee. If you want it now. If not, it could be months before we have another opening."

"And how long do I have to decide?"

"Do you really think you can spend another night alone with her in your apartment?" Melody took a napkin and wiped the blood off Dick's cheeks. "She could seriously injure you and have no idea what she was doing. Or, in self-defense, you could injure her. It's your choice. But if that's what you want to do, you'll have to sign waivers. We can't be responsible for what she might do."

"And she can move in now?"

"Immediately."

"I don't want her on tranquilizers. I don't want her medicated up. She'll still have moments of clarity. I'm sure she will. And I don't want her to lose that. I don't want her to sleep through what's left of her life."

"Within the limits of safety, we'll honor your wishes."

"Then let's do it."

Melody signaled, and the orderly started rolling the wheelchair out of the dining room, in the direction of the Alzheimer's wing. Dick started to follow but Melody stopped him.

"Not now. Later. Give us a chance to settle her in. Right now, this is harder for you than it is for her. She doesn't need you now. She has no idea what's happening. If you like, we'll call you when she wakes up. You knew this was coming. We all did. You did a wonderful job of taking care of her for as long as you did. Now it's time to pass the baton to us."

Dick returned to his seat. He didn't finish his meal. He even turned down his favorite dessert—banana split with cherry-vanilla ice cream. Then he docilely followed along when Mercy coaxed them all to a nearby TV room, which happened to be empty. She played 1960s folk songs on an old piano and they all sang along. Then she encouraged Dick to get his violin and play the classics that he loved and knew by heart. Soon Dick was telling jokes and delivering monologues from plays. Eventually, he was able to tell anecdotes about Belle and himself, from their fifty-five years of marriage. And the others joined in with stories of their own to amuse and distract him.

At dinner, Dick got word that Belle was awake, and he went to visit her. When he returned ten minutes later, his face was covered with a patchwork of band aids the nurses had insisted on, covering the scratches Belle had inflicted at lunch.

"Is she okay?" asked Abe.

"She's in good voice. Screaming and cursing as well as I've ever heard her. There's nothing wrong with her lungs. She still thinks I'm a stranger and panics when I get near her."

Mercy suggested, "Tomorrow, take a couple decks of cards. Set up a card table where she can see you, outside her room. Start playing solitaire, and when she walks your way, deal a hand for her and get a chair for her. Your minds can touch even if she can't understand a word you say. It's a way to be together and to be alone at the same time. Over time, maybe she'll let you hold her hand while you play."

Mercy played the piano again, and Abe sang along with the others. He joined in the general conversation and felt that he belonged, as if he had known these people for years. And when they broke up to go to their separate apartments and sleep, it felt natural that Mercy took his hand and led him away, perhaps to her room.

12 ~ Bundle of Joy

Mercy brought Abe back to the activity room, where she had delivered her sermon that morning. She moved the ladder from the cupola to a spot to the right of the piano where a body-size hole in the ceiling led to crawl space under the peak of the roof.

"Welcome to our secret passage," she announced, turning on a flashlight, then climbing up and in.

Abe followed her and when he poked his head through the hole, he saw the same floor as in his dream, with the same two boards removed and a quilt spread, and Mercy lying there.

"This doesn't look safe," he said. "The surface you're lying on has no support. That's the ceiling of the room below. It's liable to give way."

"That didn't happen in the dream."

"What dream?"

"The dream I had last night."

"About the two of us in a place like this?"

"You dreamt it, too?"

"This is scary."

"Hold my hand."

"But that's impossible," he insisted. "Two people can't have the same dream when they haven't had the same experiences to base it on. I've never been in a place like this before. And I've never, never—"

"Bundled?"

"Yes. Bundled. I've heard of that practice, but it died out nearly two hundred years ago, except maybe among the Amish."

"This is both absurd and romantic, don't you think? To lie side-by-side, fully clothed, with someone you think you might care for. To short-circuit society's norms and spend the night together, welcoming a meeting of the minds before the bodies meet, sharing whatever you think of, becoming truly intimate, falling asleep together, enjoying one another's presence. What a brilliant idea, and we both had it at the same time."

"But we can't stay here all night."

"And why not?"

"What about Jemmie? Aren't you your brother's keeper?"

"Cat. I asked Cat to keep an eye on him tonight. She'll sleep on the sofa in our living room."

"So you planned this?"

"Of course."

"When did you know?"

"That I wanted to lie here beside you and hold your hand all night? When I woke up this morning after the dream. It was a very good dream."

"Cat knows about this?"

"Like a confidante in an old French play. When was the last time you had a secret rendezvous? When did you do something outlandish with a lady you just met? And not for sex, but for romance, pure unadulterated romance as sweet as that scene in the dream we shared, as ten-year-olds no less. Let's be ten-year-olds tonight."

"That's mad, totally mad."

"Yes, mad, in the old sense of wild and unexpected and exhilarating. Welcome to a new world, Mr. Burgoyne, my Gentleman Johnny. Welcome to our sanctuary in the secret passage that leads nowhere. Come lie here beside me, with a two-by-four separating us. Put your shoulder on top so I can rest my head on your shoulder. I'll turn off the flashlight, and we'll hold hands in the dark, and everything we can imagine will be ours."

He lay down beside her as she had suggested and as both of them had dreamed.

When she turned off the flashlight, there was a moment of total darkness as their eyes adjusted. Then, they saw sparks of light coming through cracks in the roof, like faint stars twinkling, as they would have seen had they lain like this in a meadow at midnight, having snuck out of their respective houses for no other reason than to be alone together under the heavens on the grass with the scent of buttercups and violets. He called her Charlotte, and she called him Johnny, and they planned their elopement—parents be damned, inheritance be damned. He had a commission in the Horse Guards, a prestigious job that entitled him to wear a dashing uniform and act the part of a man of leisure, a man the ladies swooned over, the uniform of a gentleman, not a fighter. He would give that up for her. He wouldn't need to attract other women if he had her. That lifestyle would be a waste if he didn't have her. And the money he had paid for that commission he could get back by selling it to someone else. That would be money enough for them to travel to the continent and live there in style for years—years of honeymoon. And when the money ran out, he'd think of something else to do, or she would think of the solution. She was brilliant as well as beautiful, and together they would be unstoppable.

"This is scary," he said. "You don't feel like a stranger. It's as if we've always known one another, as if that dream were a memory that we shared, as if we actually played a bundling game together as kids. As if we lay under the stars and plotted our elopement; only the first time you were Mary and the second time you were Charlotte."

"And who am I now?" she asked.

"You are Mercy, formerly Mary, of Arcadia Estates in the White Mountains of New Hampshire."

"And you are Johnny, formerly Abe. And we are both young and old at the same time. We have just met, and we've always been together. And we should be cold in this unheated crawl space. It's February and a foot of snow covers the roof above us. But we aren't cold, with the warmth of our bodies nestled together. And above us we see not random spots of light, but rather stars in their proper places—the Belt of Orion, the Big Dipper, the North Star. And it's spring, and anything can happen. Two seventy-years-olds. Correction; forget that I said that. Two ageless people can fall down a rabbit hole, holding each other tight, and land some place where the laws of space and time don't apply, where the impossible is possible, and they can be crazy in love together, and their lives can start afresh together."

"Love? Did we get to love, already?"

"Shut up and enjoy the ride," she cuddled closer. "I bundled with Jim, my Jim, James Warren," she remembered, "in my parents' house in Barnstable. We did that dozens of times, whenever he came to visit. It took forever until he felt established enough to get married and we moved to Plymouth. But that bundling was romantic in a way that being naked together never reached when we were married and making children together. In that beginning, everything was possible. And later we were so caught up in the tasks of everyday living that we were always distracted, always thinking about what we had to do next and then next, and we were never completely present, in the moment, for each other.

"And it was like that with Frank, too, in another life of mine. I invited him to my apartment after a second date—a Meg Ryan movie, *Sleepless in Seattle.* I had a meal ready, having anticipated we might end up there together and hoping this wouldn't be the last date with him, but not wanting to go too fast. And I put the dinner in the microwave to heat it up, and we talked and talked some more, cuddling on the sofa. Then we cuddled on my bed, fully clothed, sharing memories and hopes, following one thread after another through the mazes of our previous lives, until words that we had always used took on new meaning as they became part of the patterns of association that we were sharing in our manic talk, our night-long high. And in the morning, never having slept, but feeling refreshed, we found in the microwave the dinner we forgot to eat the night before."

Abe rolled over and kneeled and tried to kiss her. But Mercy held him back. "Down, Rover. Not now. Not here. Don't wreck the moment."

"So, you have this thing, this inhibition, this fear of physical intimacy, perhaps a fear of nudity as well, a sense of modesty perhaps, a reborn virginity?"

"Enough, Doctor Daly. I'll not be diagnosed. Everything in due time. Tomorrow is Monday. Meet me in the drawing room at two in the afternoon and all will be revealed."

"Drawing room?"

"It's directly above the dining room."

"And why?"

"You have all these questions. Well, I have answers for you. You'll see for yourself. And bring a sketch pad."

"What?"

"A sketch pad and pencils. You can get them at the front desk. What do you think the drawing room is for?"

"I don't know what to think."

"Good. Then you have an open mind."

13 ~ The Drawing Room

Abe was the only man.

When he arrived in the drawing room, he saw a dozen ladies sitting at tables arranged in a semi-circle around a platform. Every lady had a sketch pad and pencils, the same as what he had brought with him, following Mercy's instructions.

Fanny and Nell were on the right side of the room. The only empty seats were on the left. Mercy was nowhere to be seen. There was an empty seat next to the seat he settled in.

He presumed that Mercy was running late.

When she arrived, she was wearing a regal purple robe that matched her purple hair. She stood straight and tall and walked at a ceremonial pace, barefoot. Perhaps she was going to deliver a performance—a speech from a play. Perhaps she would sing.

She ascended the platform, scanned the audience, from the far side with Fanny and Nell, slowly, till her eyes focused on Abe and she smiled. Then she tossed her wig aside and, with a shrug, she let her robe fall to the ground.

She was stark naked—sagging breasts and gray public hair, legs spread and shoulders back, striking a pose and holding it and looking straight at Abe.

This was a life drawing session, and she was the model today. They probably took turns.

Everyone was sketching quickly and intently except Abe.

Everyone took the nudity for granted—everyone but Abe.

He couldn't help but stare. By the time he opened his sketch book, she had twisted her torso to assume a second pose—this time looking in the other direction, but with her groin still toward him, the outer labia clearly visible through the tufts of gray hair.

He had never been to a life drawing class. He had no artistic talent. He had no idea what to do or how to do it. But he felt compelled to do something. It would be lewd and rude to just stare at her naked form without the excuse of drawing.

So, he put pencil strokes on paper, staring at her and paying little attention to the marks he was making. When she changed poses again, this time turning her back to him, he saw that what he had randomly drawn wasn't terrible, not realistic, but the distorted proportions gave the drawing a stylized look, as if the mistakes weren't mistakes, as if they were intended.

He turned to a fresh page and focused on her backside and the roundness, the groove, the way the curves of her buttocks flowed to the length of her legs. And from this angle, he caught a glimpse of her right breast. It wasn't sagging as he had thought at first, rather forming an interesting shape with the line of her upper arm running parallel with the top side of her breast.

Then she sat down on the platform and leaned back, arching her back, bringing her breasts up, prominent, the highest points of her body, and her legs crossed, but spread, nothing blocking his view of her pubic area. She matter-of-factly displayed everything. She was an object to those who were drawing her. She showed no sign of shame or modesty. He was free to stare as he had never in his life had the opportunity to stare at a naked woman, in the flesh, not a picture. This was much more intense than watching a stripper remove her clothes and wriggle, and dangle from a pole, and dance.

He focused on her breasts. Her lovely breasts, subject to gravity and to the demands of muscles stretched several ways at once were not cone-shaped like in some Greek statue, but thicker than expected toward the base and one nipple leaning to the left while the other leaned to the right. In this pose, one breast stood high and the other was bent to the side.

He drew, immersed in what he was seeing, becoming aware of her musculature, of the curves of flesh, without judgment, without comparison to centerfold bodies from printed copies of Playboy and Penthouse in college days, images touched up to mask irregularities — unreal realism.

This was the woman herself, in all her idiosyncratic diversity of form, her unique body to be savored from the wrinkles of her neck, to the extra fold of flesh above her hips, to the varicose veins on her legs, and her bald head reflecting the sunlight that shone through the window behind her.

She was gorgeous, uniquely gorgeous. He no longer saw any similarity with Meg Ryan.

He wanted to touch those feet, to play with those toes, to caress and then to kiss every twist and curve that he was memorizing now. As he sketched her, her complete image branded indelibly in his memory.

And silently he thanked her for this introduction to her physicality. The distance and the discipline of drawing forced him to look and to learn to see, in a way that he had never come to know any woman's body. It was impossible to know a woman's body when you are free to touch and grope and kiss, when the view of the physical shape is just a fleeting stage on the path to physical action and conjunction.

At seventy years old, he was finally learning to see and appreciate a woman's body, and not just any woman, but Mercy, who he had just met and who he had known forever. He thought how he would draw her in words. He imagined having nude models to practice writing descriptions in creative writing classes. His ideas of Mercy's age and her beauty changed as she changed poses and stretched this way and that, loose wrinkled flesh becoming tight and taut this way and that. He saw her not just as she was at that moment, but also as she had been at different ages through her life. Round bottom. Probably very much as it had been since she was a teenager. Small breasts. The feet. The hands. The neck.

What color was her original hair? The V of hair at her crotch, with the line of the opening down the middle. Did she ever shave there? Would she ever shave there in the future? Gray, but with flecks of brown, and a hint of red as well.

He guessed she had been a red head. Did she have a wig that would restore that natural look? He liked her outlandish wigs and saw them as willful and creative, self-made.

He imagined her wearing clothes from different periods like a toga or an eighteenth-century gown dressed for a ball. In his mind, he played dress-up with her as a life-size doll.

When the session ended and everyone, but Abe left, and Mercy emerged from the rest room, fully clothed, in her purple robe and purple hair. Abe was still mesmerized, remembering the curves of her naked flesh.

"Johnny?" Mercy waved her hand in front of his eyes, breaking his stare. "Are you okay?"

"Not really," he admitted. "My eyes are playing tricks on me, like with a strobe light. I see you now as this person and now as that, or overlaid one on the other, 'double exposure' you called it in your sermon. Or it's as if I looked at the sun, and now I'm seeing the afterimage. I still see you in the all-together."

"What a sweet expression—the all-together. Makes me think of a polite social occasion, a get-together. Imagine a get-together where everyone is in the all-together."

"How can you stand on a platform for two hours, stark naked, with a dozen people staring at you? Isn't it demeaning to be treated as an object, like a piece of meat?"

"You know the old adage about imagining the audience is naked as a way to get over your nervousness when speaking in public? Well, I imagine the artists as naked—you as naked."

She looked Abe straight in the eye and savored his embarrassment. Then she imagined what Abe would look like and act like in another time and place. A fine figure of a man, a true gentleman, perhaps not so naive and innocent. She was intrigued by the tension between who he was and who he could be. She imagined undressing him and then dressing him quite differently, imagined him well-groomed and supremely confident, commanding respect and obedience. A general.

"You've never exposed yourself in public?" she asked. "You've never been to a nudist colony?"

"No. But I've been to beaches on Mykonos and St. Martin where clothing was optional. A few young ladies chose the option, but I just looked."

"And you stood transfixed, staring?"

"Probably. Caught by surprise."

"Was it the surprise that caught your attention today, or did you like what you saw?"

"What I continue to see, what I can't help but see."

"And you wish that hadn't happened?"

"On the contrary. But I never expected to have such an experience in an assisted-living facility."

"It was that bad, really? You aren't used to looking at the withered body of an old lady? You were married many years; you saw your wife as she was when she was young, overlaid with images of how she looked over the years. And when you saw me, it was the shock of first exposure. As Shakespeare put it, when he went to a life-drawing class in an assisted-living facility: *Bare ruined choirs, where late the sweet birds sang.*

"We do these sessions once a month, and we take turns modelling. If you had missed me today, you would have had to wait a year to see me like that, except, of course, if you were granted a private viewing. I thought it would be a fun introduction displaying the merchandise, unadorned. A public viewing of my privates. Your constitutional right to my privacy. Forgive me, I enjoy teasing you. Your look of embarrassment is classic."

"And your look of no embarrassment is unforgettable."

"We'll probably get a big turnout next month. We haven't had a male model since I've been here. We'll have to set up more tables."

"Have you met him? "

"Who?"

"The model."

"Why that's you, of course. They're looking forward to your turn. We haven't had the opportunity to study the male form since I've been here."

"Nude?"

"Yes."

"Completely?"

"Of course," she savored his embarrassment. "Would that I had my cellphone now. I fain would catch thy look, dear sir. Unforgettable."

They arrived at dinner late, together, holding hands, and sat beside one another at their group's regular table, eating one-handed, she with her right and he with his left, though he was righthanded, so they could still hold hands.

14 ~ Mything Persons

"I followed your advice," Dick told Mercy at dinner. "When I visited the dearly remembered who can no longer remember, I set up the card table, dealt the cards, and she joined me. We played double solitaire, and she beat me, soundly. But she didn't seem to notice that I was there, even though I held her hand the whole time, much to her annoyance because she wanted to use both hands to pick up the cards and slam them down with authority. She was there, but she wasn't really there.

"I wish Jemmie could find her name, her real name, her other-world name. Like Burgoyne and Sheridan and Mercy Otis Warren and Catharine Macaulay and Nell Gwyn and Aphra Behn and Fanny Burney. All real people from long ago. Thanks to Jemmie we have these shadow selves. We're more than just old folks in an old folks' home in the White Mountains. We have within us echoes of the past. But not Belle. And now she's locked up in the Alzheimer's wing, and she's locked up inside herself.

"For me, Jemmie's naming is fun and enriching. I've been reading Sheridan's plays and that's been a helpful distraction, a way to avoid thinking about the here and now. Belle and I met while acting in an amateur play fifty years ago. And we had parts together in other plays over the years. Maybe as many as a hundred. I never counted. I never thought it would end. I thought it might be fun to stage amateur theatricals here at Arcadia. Maybe we could do a play by Sheridan or Burgoyne or Mercy Warren or Aphra Behn. But they are all dreadfully dull. The plots make no sense in terms of today's social norms. The jokes fall flat. The word play comes out as gibberish because many of those words haven't been used for hundreds of years or their meaning has changed. Most plays that were popular two or three hundred years ago fall flat today.

"But Jemmie was right giving me that Sheridan nickname. Theater is in my blood. I even wrote a play, though I couldn't convince our theater group to stage it. They wanted to stick to the classics. It was more than forty years ago that I wrote that play. Maybe it would be fun to do

Richard Seltzer

it now, at least as a staged reading, to see the characters come alive after all this time."

"What's it about?" asked Abe.

"Identity and fate. I call it 'Without a Myth'."

"Myth America," Jemmie chimed in, rocking his chair back and forth. "Mything in action. Mything persons."

"In this play, all of life is a play. And the characters have been given a script, just one script. They can take it or leave it, but that's the only free choice we will ever have. The characters have twenty-four hours to accept this script or to have no script at all. The script itself is nonsensical, with an evil magician and dragons, a deadly spell, a princess who needs to be saved, and a hero who must save her.

"While they still have a choice, a character can temporarily drop out. In that case, everyone else freezes in mid-action and that one character moves about and speaks out of script, as he tries to decide what to do.

"We see the main character, Amythos, drop out repeatedly. He's the one who is supposed to save the princess and marry her. But he rebels and asserts his independence. He says, 'This isn't my myth. This isn't my role. This isn't who I am.'

"In the script, an evil magician has cast a spell by which the princess will die unless the hero kills the dragons and then her handmaid touches her. The detail that the handmaid has to touch her seems silly and irrelevant. The whole plot is deliberately ridiculous. If you only live one life, why would you choose this one? Amythos would like to be his real self, whatever that might be. And what is anyone's real self? But if he drops out for good, he'll be all alone in emptiness, without a myth. He can indulge himself with doubts for a day, but then he has to get on with the life that was scripted for him.

"Then the girl playing the part of the princess drops out, and the girl playing her handmaid takes her place. That means that there is no handmaid, which means there will be no handmaid to touch the princess after the dragons have been killed. Hence, by the bizarre terms of the magic spell, the princess will die.

"Amythos and the actress who was the handmaid and who is now the princess talk about their options while everyone else is frozen. She can drop out and have no myth at all or she can stay in her new role and

64

die. They hope that the myth has been broken by these changes, and that hence, they will be free to be themselves. But it's likely that no one is ever free.

"It so happens that the setting is Arcadia, the original Arcadia is a mythical realm of happiness in ancient Greece. If we did a reading in the Alzheimer's wing, Belle could have a part. She could be someone who has dropped out of life, who no one notices and no one hears."

"Are you serious?" asked Mercy.

"Not really. It would be far too much hassle to do it in the Alzheimer's wing."

"But let's do a play," Nell pleaded. "It doesn't have to be a written play. We can improvise. I'm itching to act. Jemmie giving me the name of an actress got me thinking about it. And maybe he saw in me, a talent that I didn't know I have. Acting is part of my being, part of who I am, who I want to be.

"These last few nights I've been dreaming about being on a stage with everybody staring at me. I can't see them, but they see me. And I deliver lines that someone else wrote and go through actions that someone else imagined. At the same time I'm someone else—separate and unique. And aside from the pride and the praise, and a tingle of exhibitionism, I feel special. While ordinary people have just one self and one life, I have this magic-like power for an hour or two on stage. I can be someone else, can feel what it's like to be someone else. I'm not just one person. There are multiple layers of me. That's refreshing, that's liberating, that's godlike."

"Improvise, you say?" Dick caught on to the idea. "Yes, Jemmie already assigned us our roles."

"The attic has trunks of old clothes we could use as costumes," suggested Aphra.

"Clothes call!" Jemmie announced. "Last call for clothes call."

15 ~ A Cast of Aspersions

The members of the team picked up flashlights at the front desk.

"There's lots of debris lying about up there. Please watch your step," the receptionist warned. "Why not wait until morning? It would be safer. There's no rule against going at night, but that's only because no one ever wanted to. People here just don't do such things."

"We aren't just people," explained Dick. "We're the cast of a play to be."

"A cast of aspersions," added Jemmie.

During the day, the attic was bright with sunshine through many windows. But at night, that vast space, about half the size of a football field, with dozens of supporting posts, had only a single 40-watt light bulb dangling from the ceiling that threw shadows, but didn't provide much light.

Mercy, Dick, Abe, Jemmie, Aphra, Nell, Cat, and Fanny lingered at the door, scanning the space with beams from their flashlights.

Dozens of old trunks, the kind that would have been used to carry clothing and personal goods on ocean voyages, were strewn willy-nilly across the floor.

Aphra, the only one who had been there before, ventured in, opened the nearest trunk, and started tossing clothes on the floor: petticoats, dresses, wigs, waistcoats and great coats. The others hung back by the door until Aphra exclaimed, "We've hit the mother lode. There's wine here, bottle after bottle of wine. I don't recognize the labels, but the dates are from way back— 1850, 1810, 1750."

"I've heard that wines, like people, get better with age," Mercy noted with a grin.

"I have cork screws in my room," said Fanny.

"I'll get plastic cups from the kitchen," Nell volunteered.

The others ran to other trunks and threw the clothes on the floor, checking for more wine, and most of them found dozens of bottles.

Once they had the cork screws and cups and began enjoying the wine, they relaxed, and the shifting shadows became fun, rather than scary. The scavenging expedition became an impromptu party, with dress-up fun, like kids getting ready for Halloween.

"Amazing," noted Dick. "I never could have imagined drinking wine that Hawthorne or even Washington could have imbibed. Wine from the days of Mercy Warren and General Burgoyne, Fanny Burney, Catherine Macaulay, and even from a hundred years before that. Imagine, to have the same liquid run through our veins and addle our thinking that could have flowed through the veins of such people so long ago."

Abe sat beside Mercy on one trunk while they rummaged through another trunk together. He watched her gulp down half a bottle of wine and hoped that might further the cause of physical intimacy. He tried to hold her hand, but she extricated herself from his grasp to dig deeper through a stack of petticoats to find more wine.

"Don't get ahead of yourself," she told Abe. "Patience, general. Patience. Everything comes to him who waits."

"Carpe diem," he urged. "At our age, we should be thinking carpe diem, rather than propriety."

"Yes. But that doesn't mean race to the finish line. Savor the day. Enjoy every minute of it."

Mercy put a tri-cornered hat on his head. It could have been a prop in a *Treasure Island* movie. Then she replaced her purple wig with a white powdered wig, with curls that extended to her waist.

"Which do you like better?" she asked Abe.

"I like you better bald, the alien look, like you're from another planet and have superpowers."

She laughed and gave him a quick kiss on the cheek.

"When I was a kid, Halloween was my favorite holiday," Abe noted. "I would plan my costume months in advance, gathering bits and pieces, scavenging and trading for what I needed to become a Greek warrior, an Indian chief, a cowboy. I never wanted a ready-made costume, nothing store-bought. That was cheating and then you ended up looking like everybody else. Later, I put together home-made costumes for my two kids. They would express their wishes, and I'd do my best to fill them. I remember best the Pac Man and Ms. Pac Man costumes I made for them out of poster board."

Dick interrupted while delving through a nearby trunk, "The original owner of this place must have been a pack rat. He must have saved the clothes of his family and of his parents and grandparents, and even generations further back. And those clothes must have been used by and added to by theater directors at the girls' school. It helped that there was so much storage space and that it was so much hassle to haul away stuff that you wanted to throw away. It was so much easier to store it."

Dick's band-aids were gone, but he had scars on his cheeks from Belle's fingernails.

Fanny and Nell cleared a path down the middle of the floor, like a runway in a fashion show, and modelled the best outfits they were able to assemble. Fanny showed off women's clothes, and Nell dressed as a man.

"In those days, women piled on layer upon layer of clothes," Fanny explained as she seductively strolled, half-dressed. "Among the well-off, getting dressed was a major project every day, even more difficult than putting on a wedding dress and accessories today. It required one or more maids to pull tight the stays, the forerunner of the corset and later the girdle, and to fasten dozens if not hundreds of buttons, many of which were out of reach for the lady being dressed. And they changed clothes multiple times over the course of a day, for morning, for afternoon, and evening, and for inside the house and out. And this, of course, was in addition to the time consumed and the expertise required to apply layer upon layer of makeup. Hair, by contrast, was easy in that day, as it is for Mercy today, with an array of wigs to choose from."

"I believe the fashion of wigs was started by men," Cat interjected. "Back in the seventeenth century both Louis XIV of France and Charles II of England has syphilis from an early age. There was an epidemic of syphilis, and either the disease itself or the crude remedies of the time often led to hair loss. So, a bald head or patchy hair was interpreted as a sign that someone was infected, which meant embarrassment, if not social ostracism. Both Louis and Charles had their heads shaved and started wearing long elaborate wigs. Soon their courtiers, and then the wealthy, and then anyone who could afford to was wearing wigs. The women, many of whom were also infected, began to wear wigs as well, shaving their heads underneath.

"The style had the added advantage of taking care of the problem of lice, which nearly everyone had. It was time-consuming and painful to have the lice nitpicked out of your hair by your servant or maid. If you wore a wig instead, the wig could be boiled every night, getting rid of the lice with little hassle. It also turned out, though they didn't know so at the time, that lice could carry the plague. So, eliminating the lice in human hair helped reduce the incidence of plague, and when it did strike, it didn't spread as quickly or as far."

"Thank you, professor," said Fanny, with a curtsy. "You'll note that the dress is open in the front. The petticoats," she continued, raising her dress and petticoats to display them, "sometimes layer upon layer of petticoats, were not considered underwear, but rather were meant to be displayed in all their magnificence. The shift was the undermost garment, looking like a long shirt, often with drawstrings or lace cuffs at neck and elbows.

"Note the elbow-length fingerless gloves, and the shoes, sometimes silk, sometimes leather, sometimes worsted—made of yarn, for the gentlemen, who may be unfamiliar with the term. The shoes were often fastened with buckles and clasps.

"Ruffles were attached to the edge of the gown sleeves, either plain or lace-trimmed, to cover the elbows and the degree of decoration and the number of ruffles varied with fashion.

"The stays, which I'm not about to torture myself with, were meant to minimize and elongate the waist and push up the breasts. The cleavage could be displayed down nearly to the nipples, not unlike fashionable attire today."

"They did have a benefit," Cat added, "beyond the look."

"And what was that?"

"They supported the breasts and the body and promoted good posture."

"Bravo. How delightful. And probably as comfortable as the hair shirts monks wore to inflict pain on themselves and hence reduce their time in Purgatory after death. So, it had a health benefit, and I thought it was just another instance of women torturing and handicapping themselves to make themselves attractive to men, like modern women wearing tall spiked heels and Chinese women binding their feet."

"Don't get me wrong," Cat explained. "Women back then did put looks and fashion before health. The stays were an exception. What they did with cosmetics was abominable."

"Pray tell."

"They started with a heavy base meant to cover up small-pox sores and other common irregularities. They aimed for snowy foreheads and bosoms, brilliantly red cheeks, bright red lips, and jet-black eyebrows. But the foundation included large quantities of lead. And the rouge, to make the rosy cheeks, included mineral cinnabar, in other words mercury sulfide, which could lead to loss of teeth, stinking breath, copious salivation, and, in some cases, death. If one cosmetic didn't kill you, another would. The dangers were well known, but that didn't stop women from using those cosmetics. There's a passage in your novel Evelina—"

"My novel?"

"A novel by your namesake—Fanny Burney. Written in 1778, the narrator tells about a Frenchwoman who had suffered an accident. 'Her face was really horrible, for the pomatum and powder from her head, and the dust from the road, were quite pasted on her skin by her tears, which, with her rouge, made so frightful a mixture that she looked hardly human.'"

"How delightful. To conclude, if I may," Fanny continued. "The eyebrow was thin and half-moon shaped, often darkened with lead, burnt cork, or soot from oil lamps, with tapered ends, and conspicuously dark. Those who lost their eyebrows from excessive plucking glued on a pair false eyebrows made of mouse-skin.

"And many women added beauty patches, pieces of dark-colored silk, velvet, or satin, attached with glue. The darkness of those patches heightened the contrast with their artificially whitened skin and helped mask smallpox scars that cosmetics couldn't deal with. At the French court there was a whole language of beauty patches: one at the corner of the eye was supposed to mean passion; one on the forehead was supposed to be majestic; and a patch on a dimple was considered playful."

"What about fingernail polish," asked Mercy. "Did they go wild with colors?"

"Like your wigs?"

"Exactly."

"With everything else they did, I would have expected that. But no. Colored fingernail polish didn't become common until the 1920s. But that shouldn't stop us from doing what we want here and now for dress-ups and improvs. We aren't all scholars, like Cat. Why don't we take pieces from the past and use them as we see fit? I see no reason why we shouldn't have fun, mixing past and present. Why not wear colored wigs and paint our fingernails whatever color we like and make good use of the wealth of outfits we've found here, as well as the wealth of wine? Now the runway is yours, Nell."

"Ready for take-off," Jemmie saluted.

Nell laughed, "No, Jemmie. I won't be taking clothes off. This is not a strip show."

"Stars and strips forever."

"Enough, Jemmie," said Nell. "You are up next, my dear sir," she told him. "Just walk down this open space and show off how you are dressed. I did him up like Benjamin Franklin. Note the three-cornered hat, the waistcoat, and the great coat on top. I dressed myself as a man as well. I read that Nell Gwyn the actress and the mistress of Charles II, often dressed as a boy or young man for roles on the stage and to cater to the king's unique tastes. The tight-fitting breeches and long stockings showed off her best feature, her legs, which would have been hidden by petticoats."

Fanny suggested, "There are masks here as well, like they used in masquerade parties. I propose that we hold a ball tomorrow night in the activity room. A masked, masquerade ball, using what we've found here."

"Bravo," shouted Dick, and the others signified their approval with applause and cheers.

"Pick what you like from here," added Fanny. "This clothing is in remarkably good shape considering its age. If you give me your outfits in the morning, I'll ask the laundry squad to wash them all at least twice, to remove the stench of mothballs."

"Me, too," volunteered Nell. "I'll be glad to help. I have a sewing machine and can make adjustments for fit. "

The atmosphere shifted from casual curiosity to serious enterprise, as they now had an immediate goal—the masked ball having become for them the event of the season. And each sought the perfect costume, with the enthusiasm they had had as kids preparing for Halloween.

16 ~ Triangulation

The attic grew darker as one after the other of the assembled friends gathered up the pieces of their costumes and left with their flashlights.

"I guess I'll be going now," Dick said to Mercy and Abe, who were sitting beside one another on the trunk next to his. "I have what I need, and I don't want to get in the way of you love-birds."

Mercy chuckled, "Don't be in such a hurry. Have some more wine and tell us about yourself. When Belle was healthy, we didn't see much of you except at mealtimes. You seem like a newcomer now, as much a newcomer as Abe here—I mean Gentleman Johnny."

He sat back down and refilled his cup. "I feel like the odd man out here. But triangles aren't always bad."

"And what do you mean by that?" asked Abe, wishing he could have this time alone with Mercy.

"Well, triangles make me think of trigonometry, and trigonometry makes me think of surveying, and surveying makes me think of George Washington."

"Of course," chuckled Mercy, drinking wine straight from the bottle.

"Because he was good at trigonometry in school, Washington was hired as a surveyor, helping divide frontier land in Virginia into parcels that could be sold. Then, because he was familiar with frontier land, General Braddock relied on him to lead the way to Fort Pitt where they were ambushed and defeated by the French and Indians. When the Revolution began, the Continental Congress turned to Washington because of his military experience and made him Commander-in-Chief of the Continental Army. So, you could argue that if Washington hadn't done so well in trigonometry, we might have lost the Revolution."

"Your mind works in interesting ways," noted Mercy.

"Now it does, when I have the leisure to read whatever I want whenever I want. But for most of my life I was a 9-5 school administrator, and a 24/7 father and husband. There was no time for the luxury of trying to figure out what life is about. But I did manage to practice and play violin for community orchestras, and occasionally dabbled in oil painting."

"You should join our life drawing classes."

"I've heard about that. But Belle, in her moments of clarity, didn't like the idea of me staring at naked ladies. And she figured that if I went, I'd have to take my turn at modelling. And she wasn't going to allow that. Her fits of jealousy, which sometimes got out of hand as the Alzheimer's advanced, were like a caress to me. It was her way of telling me that she loved me."

"But now you can join us, right?"

"We'll see about that."

"We have a dearth of male models. We just got our first."

"Johnny?"

Abe cringed in acknowledgement.

Mercy continued, "So how did you wind up as a school administrator?"

"Back in college, I majored in philosophy, with a minor in history. I went to grad school in philosophy, not because I wanted to teach that subject in college, but rather following up on my personal curiosity, especially about the period from the end of the seventeenth to the end of the eighteenth century when it seemed possible for someone to understand everything, when a flash of inspiration could lead to a breakthrough in science or math or philosophy.

"I was fascinated by Leibniz and Swedenborg, scientists as well as philosophers and visionaries, when real science was just beginning and talented amateurs could make important discoveries, and a single individual like Newton could revolutionize our understanding of the universe. Leibniz was a rival of Newton, developing what became calculus, independently, at the same time. This is the same Leibniz who was mocked by Voltaire in *Candide*. He was the character who believed that this is 'the best of all possible worlds.' How silly that idea sounded until recently when cosmologists concluded that there have been innumerable Big Bangs. That Big Bangs happen all the time but self-destruct in nanoseconds, except for one that by chance led to a set of conditions and physical laws that made a universe that was stable. By a cosmic law of evolution, survival of the fittest, this one has lasted for nearly fourteen billion years. In other words, the universe that we live in is one of the best, if not the very best of all possible universes.

"Back in grad school I wanted to do a dissertation on how each of us is all of us. That was my own idiosyncratic take on Leibniz' notion of monads. Now all these old clothes from his era bring him to mind again and I'm is tempted to dress like Leibniz, with a sword and a gold-topped walking stick, and, of course, a great coat and a tri-cornered hat."

Mercy pressed him, "If you weren't going to teach it, what good was a graduate degree to you?"

"This was the late sixties. The draft and the Viet Nam War meant that you couldn't think about a career. Nobody would hire you for a serious job if you hadn't taken care of your military obligation. At least that was my excuse. I drifted from undergrad to grad school, staying at the same college, and with no career in mind. I was just enjoying learning, wanting more of what I had had for four years, and hoping the draft board, in the days before the lottery, would leave me alone until the war ended.

"I was a good student. Grad school wasn't costing me anything. My department paid me a stipend, which was enough to live on, given my spartan needs and interests. Then came the lottery, and my number was 310. I was home free. I celebrated and got drunk with other lucky students and woke up one morning with a lovely young lady resting her head on my shoulder and prompting me to plan the rest of my life, now that I could plan. To impress her, I told her that I wanted to give back to society, that being so fortunate as I was with the draft, I owed a debt. It would be self-indulgent and egotistical of me to stay in grad school. I said I wanted to teach in an inner-city school, elementary school, where kids were not yet formed, and you could make a difference. For a school like that, I could get an exemption from the requirement for certification. I could get a job right away and go to night school to learn how to teach.

"Belle was working on her master's in early childhood education. We believed we were fated to have met that way at that time. We planned our future together before we made love for the first time. We'd get jobs in the same school district and live together. We didn't need to get married. We didn't need a marriage certificate to hold us together. We were different from most people, and we would make a difference in the world.

"After one year of teaching in Watts, we were burnt out, discouraged, and cynical about teaching, about society, and about the future of the world. But we were still high on each other. We moved to Boston, got married, and got office jobs. We both took night courses in school administration. Education was still important to both of us. But teachers couldn't really make a difference so long as the administration was screwed up.

"Belle dropped her studies when she got pregnant. I continued. I got a job as a vice principal at a high school—a disciplinarian. I wrote a dissertation about school discipline based on my experience. I got a Doctor of Education degree. I became a principal here, then there, then somewhere else. Eventually, I became a superintendent of schools.

"We had four kids, but somehow we found time for amateur theatricals. I found time, too, for violin and piano as a hobby. The kids grew up and, with student loans and parent loans, we managed to get them through college. They married. They moved away. I retired. Finally, after a long and fulfilling life, we had time to focus on one another. We planned to travel.

"Then the first symptoms of Alzheimer's appeared. Belle would forget simple facts or things she meant to do, and she'd insist that she didn't forget, that she never forgot anything, and somehow, I was to blame. The incident of the police finding her in the middle of the night, and the diagnosis of Alzheimer's changed everything. I went from being a henpecked husband with an irascible wife to being her caregiver, a more than full-time job with no let-up, no backup, no breaks, no vacation, and never any appreciation from her because, of course, she didn't understand what was happening to her. And, no matter what I did, I was to blame for everything. That was my life until her breakdown here yesterday, and her admission to the Alzheimer's wing.

"I have no idea what happens to me now. All the weight of caregiver responsibility has been lifted from my shoulders. Yes, I can and will visit her, but she doesn't recognize me and barely takes notice of my presence, except for random and brief moments of clarity, when she panics and screams and begs me to help her escape.

"Now for the first time since college, I have time on my hands. I can read just for the heck of it and indulge in trying to make sense of the universe, like I did back in college. And here among all these costumes, I'm tempted to dress up like Leibniz or Swedenborg and pretend that I can make sense of the world and the fate of man and maybe discover the nature of the soul and of the afterlife, if there is one.

"Enough," he concluded, standing to stretch his legs, and pouring himself another cup of wine. "How did you get me to talk so much about myself?"

"I think you have the answer in your hands," replied Mercy with a smile.

"And you, as well, my dear," and he knocked his plastic cup against her bottle and took another swallow. "So, what was your career? What was your calling? What did you do with your life?"

"As if my life is over?" she asked.

"Well, tell me the prelude. What did you do before the beginning of the rest of your life, before now?"

"I've been a physical therapist, a psychotherapist, a registered nurse, a folk singer, a guitar and piano teacher, a yoga instructor, and an acupuncturist. But, at one point, I did have a calling, a true calling."

Dick laughed and transmitted a knowing look as he took another big gulp of two-hundred-year-old wine. "Let me guess. Calling, you say. Call girl perchance?"

She winked back and whispered loudly, "Phone sex."

"You mean back when you were in college, over forty years ago?" Dick knocked his cup to her bottle again, while Abe refilled his own cup and stared at Mercy in disbelief. "As if that matters now," Dick continued. "But that's intriguing, adds some spice to my idea of you, and makes me wonder about the backgrounds of these other so prim and perfect older ladies."

"No," she corrected him. "Not back in college. I had that job just five years ago. On the phone, nobody knows if you are twenty or sixty. It paid well. And it was great fun to start with. When it got repetitive and boring, I stopped."

"What the hell," Abe exclaimed, in too loud a voice. "How many selves do you have? How many people have you been? As for me, I'm uncomplicated. I'm just a retired high school teacher and a British general."

"You don't do yourself justice," Mercy consoled him, finally shifting her attention from Dick to him. "I'm sure you have more in you than that."

"Then you'll bring it all out, I'm sure," he chuckled. "With those drawing lessons, I'll probably wind up becoming the next—"

"Grandpa Moses," she offered.

Dick asked, "And that, I presume, was the pinnacle of your many careers?"

"Close. Phone sex was a creative challenge, a form of improvisation, a sub-genre of acting, where you have no script, just suggested scenarios. It was similar, in some ways, to psychotherapy. You know, catching hints of the customer's wants, including wants he never before admitted to himself; learning how to prompt him to let loose and let his fantasies unwind; turning his embarrassment and shyness into sexual tension and turn-on. But there was another venture I had fun with in the early days of the Internet. I would do voice overs and sound effects for porn videos."

"You're putting me on," Abe exclaimed.

"Do you mean I'm turning you on?" she winked. "The right words can caress the p-spot, the porn-spot in a man's mind."

"Maybe it's the wine," said Abe, "not just for you, but for me as well. I feel spaced out, like I'm not really here. I can see you, and I'm sure you can see me. But I feel distant, absent, out of it, as if I were a visitor rather than an inhabitant, not just of Arcadia, but of this world."

"Okay, Mr. Stranger in a Strange Land," she prompted him, with a superficially sexy voice. "Tell me who you really are—not just a retired high school English teacher, and not Johnny Burgoyne, either. What's your deep dark secret? What's the self you always wanted to be?"

"I'm a closet novelist," he admitted.

"Go for it, baby. Tell it all. Start with the title."

"*Breeze*, I called it. I wrote it twenty years ago. The manuscript is lost."

"And how did you lose it?" she prompted in a mockingly sexy voice.

"My wife, Babs, was a pack rat. A few months after she died, I went through the house and got rid of all the reminders of her except photos and special keepsakes. I tried to give away and ended up donating her clothes and all the bins of baby clothes and children's clothes she had kept in the basement. She couldn't bring herself to throw away anything our kids had ever used and clothes of hers from forty years ago that she would never fit in again. I threw away dozens of boxes of old school papers and bank records and paid bills. My manuscript must have been in one of those boxes I threw away, trying to escape from the past, trying to become a new person and start a new life. *Breeze* was lost, but the idea remains."

"And the story, give us the story."

"*Breeze* was based on the premise that souls can move from one body to another and from one time period to another. Not reincarnation, not the soul moving at the time of death, rather another mechanism that the main character doesn't understand. The book tells the story of a young woman from today who suddenly finds herself at Troy in the body of Briseis, the trophy slave of Achilles."

"You dared to write from the perspective of a young woman?"

"The best parts came to me in my sleep. And young women who read it said it rang true. I felt like I had tapped into something special, that I was in tune with something within me, that, like Dick said with the title of his would-be dissertation, in some sense each of us is all of us, that we have the potential in us to be other people and not just the other selves that Jemmie has labelled for us. And that's what some authors, like Shakespeare, tap into, to create characters who feel real hundreds of years later."

"Hello, Mr. Shakespeare," Mercy leaned forward and kissed him on the cheek. "Thank you for sharing your innermost fantasy. With such knowledge you have given me power over you, dear sir. You are now at my mercy. At the mercy of Mercy."

"Merci beaucoup, madame," he replied, delighted that somehow his tale had outdone Dick's, and he had once again won her attention.

17 ~ Prelude to a Party

As planned, Abe arrived at the activity room alone. Mercy would join him there. She wanted to surprise him with her outfit.

There was a full-length mirror on the wall in the hallway to the left, near the door. He hadn't noticed it before. Abe looked at himself, adjusted his cravat, which was scraping against his chin, and pushed the tip of his tri-cornered hat to what looked like a jaunty angle. Then he undid the brightly polished brass buttons of his red outer coat to reveal the brown waist-coat underneath, removed the sword from his belt, and stood sideways, leaning on his sword like on a walking stick, and with his other hand on his hip. Then he removed the hat and mimicked the commanding pose in the portrait of Burgoyne by Joshua Reynolds.

What were the odds that he would find a British general's uniform in a trunk in the attic? It certainly hadn't belonged to the original owner of this property or his forebears, as was the case with most of what they found. This must be a twentieth century replica, a theatrical costume purchased or handsewn for a play put on by the girls' school. Maybe for *The Devil's Advocate* by George Bernard Show, and hence intended as the uniform of General Burgoyne himself. The part to be played by a girl. A tall girl with a build like Abe's, who was probably recruited for it because she had a prominent nose and flat masculine cheeks like Burgoyne. She was probably mortified to be chosen for such a role and relieved that her parents and her boy-friend George, back in Swampscott, would never see her like this. The only audience would be the other girls at the school.

Swampscott? George? Where did that come from? Abe wondered. The uniform seemed to make him suggestible, made it easy for him to imagine what others would have thought and imagined wearing it.

He had added a powdered wig and a tri-cornered hat which weren't in the portrait, but suited today's idea of what people from then looked like.

He was pleased. Mercy would get a laugh out of this.

Of course the portrait, which he had seen in books in the library, had an outdoor background with menacing clouds and a landscape that might have been a scene of battle. He couldn't duplicate that. But the background he saw in the mirror wasn't the white wall behind him in the hallway. Rather, he saw a hillside, and there was movement among the bushes and trees, both left and right. Small green figures were slithering toward him through the thick grass, then stopping short and becoming still. Those weren't animals—not squirrels, not chipmunks. No, God doesn't make little mammals like that. Those were humans seen from afar, people camouflaged.

And near his feet on either side, he saw straight lines of red, made up of little figures. Men seen from afar. Line after line advanced up the hill, clearly visible. Thousands of little men wearing red uniforms, like his red uniform.

"What the hell," he exclaimed, then turned to look behind him at the plain white wall, all up and down both sides of the hallway. And when he looked back the mirror was gone, and he doubted that it had ever been there. His mind must be playing tricks on him. Dressed in the uniform of a British general from the era of the Revolution, dressed like General Burgoyne would have dressed, he had imagined the Battle of Bunker Hill as Burgoyne might have seen it in the distance. He shut his eyes to erase that phantom scene from his memory, but instead, with eyes shut, he felt the reality of that scene and the senseless stupidity of it.

Tom Gage, his old school mate and drinking buddy, was a bloody idiot. Such arrogance. Tom thought he could scare the local yokels into surrender. He presumed that the sight of an army of British regulars, advancing in well-disciplined lines, would terrify the amateurs who were facing them. Hence, he wanted his men fully exposed, clearly visible, as if they disdained whatever defense these inexperienced colonists might improvise. This ragtag set of shopkeepers and farmers, who had surprised a much smaller British detachment at Lexington and Concord, wouldn't be so lucky this time. Thanks to the cooperation of hundreds of loyalist informers, Tom knew very well what the colonists would do. He knew their weaknesses: fear, disorganization, lack of discipline. They had no experienced officers. They would make up what they were doing as they went along, like children playing a game of war. They would have no overall plan. Each man would act on his own, doing what felt right at the moment. Yes, Tom was sure they would run for it as soon as they saw line after line of red-clad British regulars advancing up the hill toward them.

Tom! Tom! Tom!

He wished that he could scream, and that Tom would hear him and change his orders.

You don't let the enemy have the high ground. And you don't line up standing tall in bright red uniforms while the enemy lies on their bellies in tall grass and among bushes and behind trees, almost invisible. With targets like this, the colonists wouldn't need to waste time aiming. Just fire, reload, and fire again in the rough direction of those advancing lines. And they could hold their first shots until the front line of this supposedly imposing army was nearly upon them, not waiting for orders, rather waiting until they could see the whites of their enemy's eyes, then all hell would be unleashed.

"Hell!" He knew enough to avoid such a mistake, from his encounters with Spanish troops and partisans in the war in Portugal two decades before. Abe knew, as Burgoyne would have known, if he actually were Burgoyne and this actually were 1775, and he had to watch from a distance, helpless to change anything, like watching a movie and, of course, unable to affect the outcome. More than half the British army dropped, dead or wounded, and yet they kept advancing, line after line, one new target after another sacrificed to British arrogance, to Tom's arrogance, and to their proud well-trained unthinking discipline.

Abe had no idea how he could have seen what he just saw and how he could have thought those thoughts.

He had thought that the centuries-old wine would ease his anxiety about Mercy and that today might be his lucky day with her—that the wine would give him confidence in his equipment, which had not been used in combat since Babs' passing, in real combat, not solitary fancy and that it might not work when needed. Maybe it could not stand and salute, much less enter into battle. Maybe this day it would wind up a disaster like Bunker Hill or he wouldn't even get far enough with her to find out. He wondered if he was delusional.

18 ~ The Masked Ball

Stepping through the door to the activity room was like stepping into a different century.

Five masked ladies in elaborate gowns, open in the front to show the petticoats underneath, and low-cut in the front to show off cleavage to the brink of indecency, sat at a table on the stage, looking through stacks of music. All the ladies were of similar build or rather, with tightened stays, looked similar. The masks covered the upper half of their faces, leaving mouth and chin clear; but even those clues didn't help. Abe didn't know which one was Mercy. Feeling as close to her as he did now, after just a few days of knowing her, he was reluctant to admit he didn't recognize her. But he knew her well enough to know that she intended to tease him and had probably primed the others to go along with the gag. Some were probably wearing high heels and some not, and heels of different heights, hidden under their long gowns, so they all seemed the same height. If he were to address Mercy by name from across the room, they'd probably all reply, enjoying a Spartacus moment. So, he would do her one better, treating each and every one of them as if she were Mercy.

Jemmie and Dick stood near the player piano at the back of the room, leafing through sheet music and music books. They didn't wear masks, but the men were so different physically that a mask would fool no one. Jemmie is short and round; Dick tall and muscular; Abe medium height and build. Jemmie was dressed like Ben Franklin, including bifocal glasses. Dick looked professorial, like Swedenborg or Leibniz.

Abe mounted the stage and looked over the ladies' shoulders. They had each brought one or more music systems and recordings to match. They were sorting through vinyl records: 78s from the 1940s; 45s from the 1950s; 33s from the 1960s; as well as 8-tracks from the 1970s; cassette from the 1980s; and, CDs from the 1990s. Music streamed from the Internet was banned here, along with cellphones. The same music had been reincarnated in different formats, each of which was supposed to be better than the last, but, for the most part, you couldn't convert what you already owned to the new format. Rather, you had to buy the same music over and over again, as one format superseded another. After you threw away the old player and its collection of music, along would come a craze for nostalgia, and you would once again buy the vinyl albums you enjoyed in your youth.

As Abe listened to their discussions about musicians and songs and albums, and about which sounded best in which format, he realized that he couldn't identify Mercy by her voice, much less by her looks.

Then Dick announced from the back of the room, "Ladies of the Arcadia, please set aside your modern music. You are not going to dance to rock or disco, much less folk music. You are dressed as genteel ladies from the Restoration and the Enlightenment, and you should dance accordingly. We have here allemandes by Purcell, Bach, and Handel, and minuets by Mozart and Haydn. Ladies line up in a row. Abe and Jemmie line up facing them. Then improvise in time to the music, holding one hand and then the other, changing from this partner to that. Let's get into the spirit of the time. Dancing isn't a matter of isolated couples. It's all one dance, weaving together everybody with everybody, like life itself."

"But you, Dick, you need to dance as well," protested one of the five interchangeable ladies. "If we use recorded music, you'll be able to join us."

"No, really. I prefer to play my violin today. I miss my Belle. She would have loved this. And playing the music, I'll imagine that she's here, that she's one of you, caught up in the spirit of the occasion, flirtatiously hiding her identity, and proud of me for my playing."

Up and down, and round and round they went, making up dance steps and maneuvers as they went along—dropping those moves that proved awkward and repeating those that worked well.

Then Jemmie sprinted to the back of the room, took the violin from Dick, pushed him back toward the ladies, and started playing square dance music and making square dance calls. "Allemande left, then do-si-do your partner."

While the music changed radically, the dance steps and patterns changed little. Square-dancing, Abe felt less self-conscious, more natural and at ease, channeling to dances back in elementary school and junior high, when he got to hold and dance with the girl he wanted to be with but who he didn't dare talk to. She would dance with him without him having to ask her or her having to accept or decline. No risk of rejection, just fun and fantasy.

After every three dances, Jemmie paused to give the dancers a rest and a chance to drink more centuries-old wine. Eventually, Abe grew bold and kissed each lady he held and twirled, and Dick followed suit. The ladies started kissing back and the kissing became part of their regular repertoire of dance moves.

When they were too tired to keep dancing, but not too tired to drink, Jemmie proposed a toast, "Let's drink to Plymouth, and to Concord, and to Lexington. Let's drink to Barnstable, to Watertown, to Winthrop, to Cambridge. But most of all let's drink to peace. May the war that began in Concord end in peace."

As the ladies left, each kissed Jemmie and Dick and Abe, dispensing tight hugs. But one, the very last, slipped her tongue between Abe's lips.

19 ~ The Clock Strikes

The night after the Masked Ball, Abe went to bed alone and dreamed he was Burgoyne, in uniform, on horseback, riding to Plymouth, to Mercy's house. He knew that Mercy's husband was away in Watertown with Washington and the Continental Army. He tied his horse to the post by the door and knocked. But Babs, not Mercy, opened the door, dressed in blue jeans and a Patriots sweatshirt.

"What took you so long?" she asked, taking him by the hand and leading him to the bedroom where she quickly stripped, then helped him, since he was taking too long.

That scene and its delightful consequences repeated again and again, until a clock in the distance struck twelve, waking him and her, Mercy not Babs, and he was sure that the clock was the one in the cupola that hadn't worked in over a century.

"What the hell?" he said out loud, then wished he hadn't and hugged her and kissed her on the neck, hoping she wouldn't take offense at such an unfriendly wake-up greeting after the intimacy they had evidently shared—if this was real and not a dream within a dream.

"Did you hear that?" she asked.

"The clock? Yes,"

"Let's face it, weird stuff is happening. I didn't come here to your room. I know very well I didn't. I dreamt I was making love with Frank, and now I wake up in your bed. That makes no sense."

"Maybe you sleep-walked. Maybe you subconsciously wanted to be with me."

"Did you lock your door last night?"

"Of course."

"Check it now."

Abe got up and looked. "It's still locked," he told her as he climbed back into bed and took her in his arms again.

"Something is bringing us together," she said.

"Isn't that supposed to be romantic? Signs that we are meant to be together? That we are fated to fall in love with one another?"

"Enough is enough. Did you enjoy Jemmie's violin playing?"

"He was brilliant."

"He never played the violin before. Not the piano, not the violin. No music lessons at all. And you heard the clock just now?"

"Yes. That's what woke me."

"And Jemmie probably heard it, too. I can imagine him crowing 'Clockadoodledoo!' But if we check at the front desk, they'll tell us that the clock is still broken and no one else heard it. When I told you about the sand in my shoes, you had a look in your eye, like you knew. The thought passed through my head that maybe you snuck into my room that night and put the sand there yourself. But no, from the look in your eyes, you didn't do that. The more likely explanation was that something similar had happened to you. Us finding sand in our shoes when we hadn't been near sand, except in our dreams, which we shared, was cute and mysterious. But now my waking up in your bed, in your locked apartment, that is over the top, like that silly play of Dick's. Like somebody wrote us into this story."

Abe laughed and tickled her tummy, triggering her laughter.

"You are fated to laugh, my dear," he intoned in a mock-ominous voice. "It's out of your hands. You are in my hands."

His hands roamed up and down, around and in, and she reached back in total abandon.

"I surrender, general," she moaned, then pulled him closer and deeper. "Do with me what you will."

"My dear, we have been granted not just one, but two lives. And in both it appears that we are fated to be together. What could go wrong?"

20 ~ Ring Around the Rosie

"Belle wants to die," Dick announced at breakfast. "I've been up with her all night. The nurse on duty alerted me. Belle refused to eat and when they put an IV in her arm, she ripped it out. She has an iron will. She can't remember. She can't think like a normal person. But she can *will*. They tried the IV again while I was there. One nurse with the needle, another nurse and I holding her arm. She kicked me and the nurse who was holding her across the room and slugged the one with the needle. They tried tying her down and strapping her arm to the bed rail. But she ripped the bed rail off and swung it as a weapon. She won't let them get close enough to give her a tranquilizer shot, and they don't have a tranquilizer gun like the ones used to capture wild animals.

"The staff won't go near her now. If anyone is going to get her to eat, it will have to be me. But she won't say a word to me—her teeth are clenched tight shut. She glares at me like her eyes are lasers firing hot hate at me.

"They say she might last three to five days without food before her systems start shutting down. They say I need to accept the fact that she wants to die. They want me to call in hospice to help ease the end. With morphine and the right words of comfort, she can pass away without pain."

He looked at a scrap of paper in his hand. "This is the number I'm supposed to call for hospice. Medicare will pay for it, they say. Medicare, which offered next to nothing in terms of therapy to help stop her from getting to this point, is happy to do anything to help her die peacefully."

Cat took his arm and helped him to his feet. "You need rest," she said, leading him away. "You're in no condition to make a decision like that. Lie down. Listen to your favorite music. Try to sleep. Later is plenty soon enough."

"We'll be there with you," Fanny called after them. "You shouldn't have to go through this alone. She's one of us. We'll all be there to help her."

***

When Dick woke up, the Ladies of Arcadia, wearing costumes from the attic, were waiting at his bed-side—new ones with new colors, but from the same era. Nell was in red, Mercy in blue, Cat in green, Aphra in black, and Fanny in orange. Fanny carried a basket. Jemmie and Abe were dressed as they had been for the ball and they helped Dick into his costume.

Together, they proceeded slowly toward the door to the Alzheimer's wing. Beside the door hung a framed list of The Alzheimer's Bill of Rights, including the right to a world of your own. Dick, the only one who had ever ventured here before, tapped in the code, which was clearly posted beside the lock.

The door opened and on the other side was an identical lock and the same instructions. Anyone competent enough to read the instructions and enter the code was well enough not to be restrained and should not be housed here.

The space smelled of soap, air freshener, and disinfectant, with lingering hints of vomit.

Dozens of shriveled, immobile, barely living bodies in wheelchairs were lined up and down the hall.

They passed open doorways where residents lay catatonic. Here and there they heard shrill screams and swearing, and stream-of-consciousness gibberish punctuated with shit and fuck.

Belle was alone, awake, glaring at the doorway as if daring anyone to enter and try to stop her from starving herself to death. The broken bed rail still dangled from her left wrist.

With the ease of an experienced nurse, Mercy unlocked the bed wheels and rolled the bed away from the wall so they could make a circle around Belle. She started them walking, then skipping in a circle, singing "Ring around the rosies, pockets full of posies; ashes, ashes, all fall down." They all sat on the floor. Then they got up and did it again as they might have at a birthday party when they were children. Over and over again they went through their dance and song. Belle followed them with her eyes, then moved her head to watch, then moved her lips as if trying to sing along.

Fanny opened the basket and gave everyone a plastic cup, including Belle. Then she opened one wine bottle after another, filling then refilling everyone's cup. And Belle, like everyone else, drank and drank again. After the third cup, she relaxed, breathing deeply and peacefully.

Then they dressed her in petticoats and a bright purple eighteenth century gown. Rather than put up a fight, Belle stroked the cloth, fascinated by its texture and color.

21 ~ Stolen Past

Abe fetched metal folding chairs so the group could sit by Belle's bedside. They held hands again as if, when they were connected, their good wishes would be amplified.

Dick stood in the doorway, leaning against the wall. "I wish she could see this, really see this," he said. "I wish she could know what's going on, what you're doing for her. You're like family to her, though you never knew her when she was her true self, when she could remember and laugh and love."

Dick broke out in laughter, almost hysterical waves of grief. Cat and Nell helped him into a seat and joined hands with him, making him part of the circle.

"Thank you. Thank you for what you're trying to do," he managed to say. "But she's gone. Thanks to you, her body may keep going. But she's gone already; she's close to brain dead, like the empty shells you see in wheelchairs in the hall. There's no way to reverse what has happened to her. You are a host of angels, not a coven of witches. There is no magic—not here, not anywhere. But she would have loved to play dress-up like you do, to live in a shared make-believe world rather than be shut up in a world of her own, irretrievably alone. And the era you chose for this make-believe, that Jemmie somehow chose for us, would have been perfect for her.

"Belle grew up an orphan and discovered her family late in life, just five years ago. Then she became obsessed with genealogy, making a connection with her family's past. As her personal memory began to fade, the distant past became more important to her.

"From her adoptive parents, she knew that some unknown woman, presumed to have been her unwed mother, had dropped her off at a safe haven fire station. Now, from her DNA and a note in a genealogy book, it appeared that those involved in the kidnapping had meant to sell her but had panicked and left her at that fire station two states away.

"Her adoptive parents had been on a waiting list for over a year, wanting to adopt a newborn. They might have stayed on that list for years to come. But they got priority because he was a fireman on duty when she was left in a blizzard, and he and his wife provided emergency foster care until the storm passed several days later. Nobody made a connection between this baby and a kidnapping hundreds of miles away that they had never heard of. The abandonment of a baby at a fire station was not a police matter. There was no investigation.

"I got Belle started looking for her origins without having any idea where it would lead, if to anywhere at all. I had her take DNA tests with ancestry.com and 23andme. Through that, we uncovered an uncle and a couple of first cousins. And from contacting them we found a genealogy book that mentioned her parents and their marriage and their only daughter having been kidnapped from the hospital the day she was born and never found.

"After a start like that, discovering a vast extended family with ancestors going back hundreds of years was a revelation. Of course, she loved her adoptive parents and their family. But suddenly she had a second identity, a second life, with connections extending deep into the past.

"I did what I could to encourage her new-found interest. I did research for her and got her into the DAR and the Colonial Dames and filled our house with antique furniture and other artifacts from colonial days.

"Because her grandfather's middle name was Powhattan, she became obsessed with trying to prove that she was descended from Pocahontas. She fantasized that if she could prove she was part American Indian she could claim a share of casino profits. Nonsense. It was all nonsense. But the research I did for her led me to scores of little-known historical anecdotes that I relished, including the story of Grace Sherwood, a Virginia witch, who she actually is descended from."

22 ~ Sewing Circle

A lady in a dark blue pants suit—Margaret, deputy director by her name tag—appeared at the door of Belle's Alzheimer's room, arms akimbo, face stern. She was about fifty-years-old, with short red hair showing gray roots. She had a clipboard in hand.

"Good morning, ladies and gentlemen. The nursing staff has asked me to read you the riot act." Then she lost her authoritative demeanor, giggled, and leaned on the door jamb for support.

"You are very creative, and you get an A-plus for effort," she continued. "Your costumes and camaraderie have livened up the assisted-living unit, improving the morale of the entire community. I don't want to do a thing to constrain your theatrical antics there. But please keep in mind that the Alzheimer's wing is a medical facility, and different standards of behavior must prevail here. Imagine the possibility that a state inspector should show up, unexpected, to find the lot of you here, masquerading as if this were Patriot's Day in Boston and you were hired entertainers in period costume. Only this isn't Boston, and you aren't entertainers, and you shouldn't be changing a patient into clothing that it would be hard for the nurses to deal with in an emergency. Our nurses have to deal with multiple emergencies every day. Hospital gowns are practical. Petticoats are not. And wine no less. You, Mr. Thor, should not be pouring wine down the throat of a patient here. What you do when you roll your wife out in a wheelchair for an excursion to other parts of the facility is your own business."

"But wine could be good for her. It's nourishment and liquid, and she takes it willingly."

"That's all very well. But wine is strictly forbidden here in the Alzheimer's wing, by the rules. No alcoholic beverages. The rules must be adhered to."

"Morphine yes, but wine no?"

"Precisely. You'll get wine stains all over the sheets and the bed itself. Can we say that the party is over now and that it won't be repeated? Can you please fold up the chairs, push the bed back in place, and put her back in her johnny?"

"Can I hang pictures on the walls?" asked Dicki.

"Certainly not. You wouldn't hang pictures on the walls of a hospital room, would you?"

"Well, what about these?" he asked, reaching into the top drawer of the dresser and pulling out a stack of cloth. "These are embroideries, antique artifacts that Belle delights in. At least she used to delight in them when she was herself. They are small and light and could be held up with scotch tape."

"Nothing on the walls. We have to spray the walls with disinfectant at least once a day. There are reasons for the rules and the rules must be obeyed. Nothing on the walls. Now please leave, or if you insist on trying to entertain her when she hasn't a clue what you are doing or who you are or even who she is, then do it elsewhere, please. Roll her out in her wheelchair; maybe take her to the activity room and resume your frolicking there. Just be sure to roll her back here and get her back into her johnny and into bed by 7 p.m. That's when visiting hours end.

"So please break this up now. Promptly. We don't want to upset the other patients. They are confused enough as it is. Routine is important for them. They need the security of the familiar and the expected. That's their only comfort in a world that, to them, is unknown and scary, and incomprehensible."

As soon as Margaret left, Fanny took the stack of embroidered cloths from Dick, and began flipping through them.

"They're from colonial days," Dick explained. "I bought them on eBay. When Belle was her old self, she showed them off at DAR meetings. They depict scenes from the Revolutionary War and everyday life at that time.

"Amazing," Fanny exclaimed and passed them around to the others. "A quilt. We can make them into a quilt to serve as a wall-hanging for the activity room, like a medieval tapestry. We'll connect these pieces and add new ones that we embroider ourselves. We'll hold a sewing circle, not here in this dismal room, but rather in the activity room. It will be a project for all of us, a project that might catch Belle's attention. Dick, you can wheel her there each day. We'll all dress in our historic garb. And we can gather props from the attic and backstage—antique chairs and other furniture and spinning wheels—I saw a few spinning wheels in the attic. Us sitting together sewing will be like a scene from the days of the Revolution, an improv like we said we wanted to do."

Mercy added, "It will be like a gathering of a Committee of Correspondence, where would-be rebels would alternate sewing, and writing and copying letters, weaving the interests of the colonies together, creating awareness that they should form a single nation."

"That's the spirit," Dick noted with enthusiasm. "Let's start today. There's no need to wait."

Together, they lifted Belle into her wheelchair, still attired in her bright purple gown.

As they rolled Belle to the activity room, Cat spoke to Mercy, "Jemmie was alone last night."

"How do you know that?"

"I woke up to the sound of him crowing like a rooster. He was wandering the halls. I calmed him down and got him back to bed. I spent the rest of the night on the sofa in your apartment, like I did the night before. I understand you have your needs, and you need to have a life of your own and not just be your brother's keeper, but please give me warning."

"I'm sorry, oh so sorry. It wasn't planned. It just happened. And it won't happen again."

"No need for that. Don't get me wrong. Your sofa is comfortable and I had an amazing dream there last night. I was Demi Moore making out with Ashton Kutcher. A very vivid dream."

Dick overheard and laughed. "That's your inner Macaulay coming out."

"What?"

"Catharine Macaulay, your other self. As a 47-year-old widow, an esteemed historian, she married the twenty-one-year-old William Graham — a Billy the Kid, if you will. It was scandalous, far more scandalous than something like that is today."

"Yes, I've read that story, too. And I, too, in the present day married a much younger man. But now I'm a good deal older than I was then. I'm not likely to find a young man here," she chuckled. "In any case, I'll keep an eye on Jemmie tonight. No problem. But I can't do it every night. And you need to alert me when I'm needed."

23 ~ Amazing Grace

The activity room still had the decorations from the masked ball. Mercy added sandalwood incense. Abe and Dick fetched spinning wheels from the attic. Cat and Aphra scavenged antique chairs from TV rooms and lounges around the facility and arranged them in a circle on the stage.

Jemmie got the player piano started with scrolls of hymns.

They drank old wine.

Fanny and Nell provided needles, thread, embroidery hooks, and pieces of fabric and instructed the others, including Abe and Dick, in the basics of embroidery. "First, make a backstitch for straight lines. Then insert a threaded needle through the back until the knot is up against the back of the fabric. Then pull through until the thread is taut."

Belle watched silently, intently, her hands fidgeting.

Fanny stood behind her, put a piece of fabric in an embroidery hoop and had her hold it in her left hand. She put a needle and thread in her right hand. Then she helped Belle, patiently, stitch by stitch, telling her what to do with words, while guiding her fingers and hands.

Belle let Fanny do as she wished, without opposition and without engagement, staring blankly across the room, never glancing down at the work.

After an hour, Fanny took a break, stretching her arms and drinking wine. When she returned to her task, she was surprised to find that Belle's hands were still at work, going through all the moves mechanically, as if from habit, without the need to look. The others, noticing Fanny's look of shock, stopped their work and stared.

Belle wasn't following the pattern sketched on the fabric, a house on a hill, but the stitches weren't random, either. Stroke by stroke the image appeared of a cow, all in one color because she only had one color of thread, but unmistakably a cow.

Then Jemmie turned off the scroll on the player piano and began playing himself, loudly, and singing along "Amazing Grace."

Belle let the embroidery fall in her lap, and her lips moved, mouthing the words of the hymn.

From her stream of mumbling sounds, words and sentences emerged, "Aye, Mr. Gisburne, but if I had the powers of Satan, surely I would not waste them in bewitching thy hogs and cotton. Surely, I'd be a witless witch to do such a thing, with nothing for me to gain from it. And Mr. Barnes, why in the name of heaven should I want to ride thy wife instead of a horse, thy fat old wife on her hands and knees, and where would that get me? And I escaped through a keyhole in the shape of a black cat? Lordy, and how much whiskey hast thou drunk today? If I were a witch, and I'm not saying I am a witch, I'd do far better with my powers than that, and thou wouldst never know I was doing it either, thou canst be sure. Witches, real witches, if there were real witches, would never be caught. The fact thou thinkest that I am one is good reason to believe I am not."

Dick chuckled, "Grace, yes, Grace, as in Grace Sherwood, Belle's ancestor. These are details I read to Belle from the research I did for her."

She fell silent again, and focused attention on her embroidery, holding the fabric high so sunlight streamed through it. She smiled in satisfaction at her work.

Then Jemmie once again played and sang "Amazing Grace," and Belle once again put down her embroidery and spoke as if to someone standing in front of her. "Luke Hill, thou art a lying thieving drunkard. A fine neighbor thou art. Thou art not about to get my land by calling me a witch. *Dalton's Country Justice* indeed. As if a law book can lay down rules for how to tell a witch from a law-abiding citizen. As if matters of the spirit world can be put to the test by ordinary mortals. Do not provoke me. Drop thy damned lawsuit, fool, or one day thou mayst wake up and learn what real witchcraft can do to thee. If thou believest, as thou claimest, that I'm a witch, thou shouldst tremble and beg, and do whatever thou canst to get in my good graces. Bringing suit tells me thou dost not think I have the power to get back at thee, tells me thou wouldst lie to seize my property. But I'll wager thou art not sure what I can and cannot do. And thou shouldst back off whilst thou canst."

Once again, she froze, silent, and stared blankly straight ahead.

"Dick, what happened to the real Grace Sherwood?" asked Abe.

"At a time when people in Virginia, unlike Massachusetts, didn't believe in witchcraft, Grace was charged with it twice in 1698. Nothing came of those charges. Then in 1706, her neighbor Luke Hill, brought another suit, and a trial was held. The justice of the peace in Princess Ann County and his fellow judges didn't want to have anything to do with the case, but they followed the book *Dalton's Country Justice*, which was intended as a guide for magistrates with no legal training. They put her to the tests described there. They had a jury of twelve women examine her naked body, and those women found strange tit-like things on parts of her body where they shouldn't be. So that court sent the case on to the highest court in Virginia, in Williamsburg, which sent it right back to them saying they needed more details.

"The local court, following the book, gave her a dunking in a pond. They postponed that test due to heavy rain, not wanting to endanger the health of the accused. Then when the rain stopped, they took her out in a rowboat, to a spot where the water was deeper than her height. They tied her up and weighted her down and let her over the side, being careful to prevent her from drowning. The book said that if she sank, she was innocent, and if she floated, she was guilty. Much to the dismay of the judges, she floated.

"So, they assembled another jury of women, this time five of them, to examine her naked body. And these women found on her private parts two things like tits of a black color. They sent the case back again to the court in Williamsburg."

"And what happened there?" asked Abe.

"Nobody knows. The records were destroyed during the Civil War. But Grace lived another 27 years, dying in 1733. She left her estate to her three sons."

"So now Belle has a name like the rest of us," added Mercy. "Grace Sherwood. Welcome home, Grace, our Amazing Grace."

24 ~ Future Dream

That night, Abe and Mercy went to bed together in Abe's apartment, deliberately, for the first time, and cuddled, and fell asleep in one another's arms.

When Abe, as was normal for him, woke up three hours later and needing to urinate, he told Mercy his dream. "We were in college. We had met in art class, drawing nude models. We had talked and eaten together in the dining hall. We had danced together at mixers. We had held hands and kissed and petted, but always fully clothed. Now for the first time, we were alone together in your bedroom."

"Yes, I saw it, too," confirmed Mercy. "There was a Beatle's poster on the wall."

"And a mechanical typewriter on the desk," added Abe. "I think it was the 1960s."

"I wanted to turn the lights out, and you wanted them on."

"I wanted you to take your clothes off first."

"And I wanted you to go first."

"Then we agreed that I would undress you, then you would undress me."

"Then we heard a resounding laugh."

"And our clothes dropped to the floor, and our bodies were old and wrinkled."

"But that didn't matter to us. We gazed at each other and caressed, then made love, on the floor, in too much of a hurry to walk two steps to the bed."

They fell asleep again and dreamed that they had been married for fifty years. And as an anniversary gift the gods gave them a magic bed, such that whenever they were in that bed together, they both had the bodies of twenty-year-olds.

They slept again and woke again. This time they dreamt they were both in their seventies and living in an assisted-living facility, Arcadia, and Mercy was pregnant—like Sarah the wife of Abraham getting pregnant at the age of ninety. Doctors were shocked. This couldn't happen.

Abortion was the only choice. Childbirth was far too risky. But this was a miracle, and you don't undo miracles.

On the other hand, Medicare wouldn't pay for prenatal care or for childbirth, or for any care the baby needed. There were no provisions for dealing with the impossible.

Then they won the lottery. One miracle saving another.

Mercy spent most of her pregnancy resting in bed and reading, Abe at her side. It was a normal, trouble-free birth. A son. They named him Whitemore, Wit for short.

They left Arcadia. An old folks' home was no place to raise a baby.

With the rest of the lottery money, they bought a house in Plymouth, Massachusetts, on the site where the Warren house once stood.

They slept and woke again. This time they dreamt that they were both as old as now, but they didn't feel they needed the services of assisted living. They felt that their lives were just beginning, not ending. They learned that if they shopped well and got last-minute discounts, they could go on world cruises for less than a hundred dollars a day. For less than what they paid at Arcadia, they could cruise continuously with food and entertainment included. They could dance until midnight every night and explore exotic places they had never seen before. They were in the middle of a tango lesson on the Piazza deck when they woke again to the sound of an ambulance pulling into the parking lot, and then a stampede in the hall outside their door.

Dick had had a stroke.

25 ~ Dick's Stroke

A maintenance man walking by Dick's apartment at six in the morning had heard a scream and found Dick on the floor. He had immediately called 911.

The EMTs wanted to know when the incident had occurred. If the stroke was caused by a clot rather than by bleeding, treatment within a couple of hours could zap the clot, and full recovery was likely. Administered later than that, such treatment could kill him. The maintenance man didn't know if it had happened that morning or the night before. Maybe Dick had been on the floor all night, unconscious and had just regained consciousness in the morning. Without unequivocal knowledge of the time of the stroke, the doctors couldn't give him the treatment.

That afternoon Margaret, the deputy director, arranged for a shuttle van to take the group to see Dick at Speare Memorial Hospital in Plymouth, New Hampshire, half an hour away.

They arrived in full costume and brought Dick's costume as well, in hopes of cheering him up. But he was in much worse shape than they had imagined.

The left side of his brain, which controls rational thought and controls the right side of his body, had been severely damaged. His right arm and right leg were paralyzed. He couldn't talk. He couldn't write. Doctors couldn't determine what, if anything he might be thinking. He didn't respond to simple questions, not even with a gesture like a wave of his hand or a blink of his eyes. They deemed him incompetent, with little brain function. He might live for years, but, if so, he would be little more than a vegetable.

A week later another ambulance returned Dick to Arcadia, with no sign of improvement.

The administration put him into the nursing home section of Arcadia and wanted to contact his relatives to come and clear out his apartment, which they would rent to someone else.

Since he couldn't speak and couldn't communicate in any way, he couldn't make legally binding decisions, and the administration was authorized to make decisions for him. By contract, he had a right to a space in the nursing home, and there was an opening for him now. From the perspective of the administration, there was no reason to hesitate. They had dealt with situations like this many times before.

The group, led by Mercy, wanted to take responsibility for Dick so he could continue to live in his own apartment. At the very least, they wanted the administration to hold off for a week, in hope of recovery. They imagined he might get better and find that he had lost his apartment and all his worldly goods were gone.

Margaret, the deputy director, laughed. "Recovery is impossible. But to humor you, we will hold off on clearing out his apartment for a week. In the meantime, we will keep him in the nursing-care wing, where he can get 24/7 care. The group of you, as friends of his, can wheel him out during the day and do whatever you think might help. Then after we have disposed of his apartment, and he is permanently settled in nursing, you can, of course, continue to visit with him, whenever you like, and wheel him over to the assisted-living side when you like. But the sooner you accept the inevitable, the better. That will help him to sense from you, even with his diminished mental capacity, that this is the way things are and must be from now on."

They dressed him in his costume and rolled him in his wheelchair to the activity room. They gave him one cup after another of the old wine. They tried aroma therapy, with one incense after the other. They also tried group breathing exercises and meditation and prayer. They rolled Belle to the activity room at the same time, parked her beside Dick, and entwined their hands; but neither responded to the other. Then Jemmie had one of his flashes of almost clarity and repeated over and over: "Right brain, right stuff; left brain, left stuff; right left, right left; the right stuff."

"Musicophilia, of course," concluded Mercy. "The book by Oliver Sacks, the neurologist and brain surgeon. The right brain/left brain thing, like *Drawing with the Left Side of Your Brain*. The left brain controls the right side of the body and the right brain the left side of the body. That's Dick's problem. He was a very rational person and the left brain was dominant. We need to wake up the right brain, the creative side. He played violin and piano so there's potential there. Maybe we can stimulate him with music and get the right brain to do some of what the left used to. According to Sacks, music occupies more areas of our brain than language does. He recounts case studies of people suffering from strokes and even from brain-damaging lightning strikes, like Jemmie, who have been helped by music therapy. It didn't work with Jemmie, at least my attempts didn't work. But maybe it will work with Dick. Sacks tells of stroke patients who couldn't speak who learned to sing basic commands.

"There's a TED talk by Jill Bolte Taylor, a scientist who was studying the brain when she had a stroke that left her like Dick, unable to walk or talk. She explains that the two halves of the brain are completely separate from one another and operate very differently. Each hemisphere thinks about different things, cares about different things, and has a different personality. The right brain focuses on the present moment: right here, right now. It thinks in pictures and learns through the movement of the body. The way she describes it, with the right brain, information streams in through all of our senses and explodes into an enormous collage of what the present moment looks like, smells like, tastes like, feels like, and sounds like. She says that through the consciousness of our right hemispheres, we are all connected to one another as one human family. We are whole and perfect and beautiful.

"The left brain thinks linearly and methodically. It deals with the past and the future. It takes the collage of the present moment and picks out details, and details about those details. It categorizes and organizes information and associates it with everything we learned in the past and projects all of our possibilities into the future. It thinks in language and connects our internal world with the external world. It remembers the chores we need to do and shouts 'I am.' That's the part of Dick's brain that was zapped when he had his stroke.

"But Jill Taylor's right brain remained strong and once she was no longer constrained by her left brain, she felt like she had found Nirvana. She pictured a world filled with beautiful, peaceful, compassionate, loving people. And she realized that the experience of her stroke was a gift that gave her insight into how we can live our lives.

"She was lucky. An operation removed a golf-ball-sized clot from her brain and eight years later she was completely recovered and delivering speeches about what had happened to her and what she had learned.

"I don't believe that Dick will be that lucky. But we might be able to, through music, wake up the power of his right brain so he can reconnect with the world and experience the kind of euphoria and insights that Jill Taylor did."

26 ~ Music Therapy

On the first day of the music therapy project, Mercy and Abe rolled Dick in his wheelchair up the side ramp onto the stage in the activity room. Belle was there already with the sewing circle. Everyone had a bottle of wine. The quilt, with its growing collection of patches was pinned to the stage curtain. A vintage boom-box was playing "Get Me to the Church on Time" from *My Fair Lady*, and Jemmie was dancing an improvised jig.

Mercy sat in front of Dick holding his hands and looking him straight in the eye. She hummed the tunes from *My Fair Lady* as they were heard from the boom box and coaxed Dick to hum with her. When he made a random noise with his lips, she applauded and praised him. He did it again and smiled with his eyes, pleased that she was pleased. By the end of the first day, he was able to hum a note after her that was approximately the same note as hers.

On day two, Mercy rolled him up to the piano. She struck a key, then held his left hand, extended his index finger and guided him to strike that same key. After doing that dozens of times with the same key, she released his hand, nudged his elbow and he struck that key on his own. That process morphed until she would strike a random key and he would then strike the same key.

On day three, she taught him to play a sequence of two, three, sometimes even four notes, following the pattern that she played.

On day four, she had him practice the same patterns of keys, only this time she sang along with each pattern becoming a voiced command: thirsty, hungry, scratch me. At first, he ignored her singing. Then, unexpectedly, Belle, up on the stage thirty feet away, responded to one of Mercy's prompts singing back "thirsty" with the same tune, and Dick echoed Belle's response. After that, Dick echoed whatever brief set of words Mercy sang.

On day five, she added nouns like water and candy and put them together with the commands which they continued to practice, making mini-sentences like "thirsty water" and "hungry candy," and he sang along, mimicking the sounds she was making; and sometimes what he mouthed was intelligible as the words she intended.

On day six, she extended the vocabulary of commands he could sing and improved the intelligibility. She also had him practice holding a felt-tip pen in his left hand. First, she tried to get him to imitate marks that she made and copy letters and words from a newspaper. Then she wrote his name and had him copy that. Then she found samples of his writing in his room and had him copy those. Soon he was able to copy any word or phrase from a newspaper. But he couldn't write a word when she said it. He had to see a written or printed word and copy it.

On day seven, Mercy invited Margaret to a recital of Dick's newly learned communication skills. She wrote his name, and he wrote his name. She highlighted a word in a newspaper, and he wrote that word. She sang "thirsty water" and other command phrases and he responded with an intelligible approximation.

"You see," she proudly announced. "He can both speak and write."

"Congratulations for what you have accomplished in such a short time. But what he is doing is simple mimicry. He can sing the word *turn*, but he has no idea what it means. If you say *turn* or write the word *turn*, he can repeat what you said and copy what you wrote, but he has no idea that you want him to do something, much less what it is that you want him to do. What you are doing is like teaching a parrot or programming a robot. He can't initiate a thought. He can't think something, anything, and say it. He can nod or shake his head to copy what you are doing. But he can't do so of his own volition to signify yes or no or anything else. He can't say that he is hungry or thirsty, except repeating what someone else says. And he will never be able to. That's the sad fact that you have to come to terms with. Believe me, I've seen dozens of cases like this over the years. I've seen excitement at little victories like yours today, and the disappointment when it becomes clear that the loved one no longer has the power of independent thought, that he is really gone, and nothing can be done about it. You get an A for effort. But you have to admit that you have failed. I should call for an orderly to take him back to his room."

"Not yet, please. We still have more than an hour before 7 p.m.. Miracles can happen."

Margaret laughed, not with bitterness, but rather with sympathy. "I, too, would like to believe in miracles, and I wish all the best for Mr. Thor."

After Margaret left, Mercy struggled to get Dick to respond, by any set of signals, yes or no to the simplest of questions. But he would only shake or nod his head in imitation of what she was doing.

Mercy gave up and started rolling Dick back to his room in the nursing section. Abe was behind her, rolling Belle back toward the Alzheimer's wing. Jemmie and the other ladies followed them in a sad and solemn procession.

As they passed the TV room, someone was watching "The Miracle Worker," with Anne Bancroft and Patty Duke. Mercy halted and grabbed the remote control from the resident who was watching. She fast-forwarded to the water scene where Anne Sullivan pours water on Helen Keller and says "water," and Helen says "water" and realizes that the sound has meaning and what it means is what she feels.

Dick, seeing that scene, broke out in tears. Mercy wiped the tears from his face and then touched them to the back of his hand singing "water." Then Dick reached up, touched tears on his cheek and sang "water." His eyes smiled.

Mercy filler a paper cup with water from a cooler in the corner and gave it to Dick. He drank a gulp, then poured some on the back of his hand and sang "water" before she could.

Mercy raced to get Margaret before she went off duty and headed home.

Margaret reluctantly followed, listened to an explanation, and witnessed a replay of Dick drinking water, then pouring some on his hand and singing "water."

"So, the parrot has learned a new trick," she admitted. "But he's still a parrot. He's doing what he's doing by rote. Yes, he isn't copying something he just heard or saw. He has learned a pattern, and he's repeating that pattern. He's like an actor who has learned his lines, not like someone who is thinking for himself."

Again, Dick said "water" and gestured with his left hand, pretending there was a cup in his hand and that he was drinking. Mercy handed him a new cup with water, and he drank that and sang "thank you."

Margaret shook her head and started to turn to walk away, when Dick took pen and paper from Mercy and with his left hand, slowly and awkwardly, but legibly, he wrote "thirsty thanks for water"

Margaret asked, "What's your name?"

And he wrote his name.

She asked, "What year is this?"

He wrote, "2019."

She asked, "Who is the president?"

He wrote, "Trump idiot," and smiled with his eyes.

Margaret conceded that he could move back to his apartment so long as his friends made a commitment that someone would be with him every minute of every day and they sign a disclaimer that they would be responsible for him. They could work out among themselves who would do what when. But he had to be attended to by them, not by staff, at all times, if he was to stay in assisted living.

Mercy followed up, "Before you go, I'd like to make one more appeal."

"And what more can you want?"

"Belle."

"Are you kidding? You're not going to convince me that she's competent."

"Of course not. But she's calm and manageable when she's with Dick, and she raises hell when he's forced to leave at night. Also, you're admitting that Dick is competent, that he can make decisions. And you need his permission to keep her in the Alzheimer's wing. Dick," she asked, "do you want Belle to stay in the Alzheimer's wing?"

"No," he sang, and he wrote "Home bring her home."

27 ~ Casanova

Dick and Belle could now sleep together. Jemmie slept on their living room floor on an inflatable mattress. Cat, Fanny, Aphra, and Nell took turns sleeping on the sofa nearby. That freed up Mercy and Abe to spend their nights together. Mercy's role in caring for Dick was her continuing music therapy.

Cat took the first night. She said she was willing to do it every night—no need to trade off. She had been having delightful dreams while keeping Jemmie company and would be happy to do that every night. She was dreaming about William Graham, the second husband of her namesake Catharine Macaulay, her Billy the Kid. In the dreams, he was a "sexy morsel," as she put it. But the others insisted on doing their part.

Aphra took the second night. She had researched her name-sake in the library and had been intrigued by what Virginia Woolf said about her in *A Room of One's Own*, praising Aphra Behn as the first woman to make a living as a writer, saying "All women together ought to let flowers fall on the tomb of Aphra Behn." Woolf also noted with disgust that a critic who was also a bishop had concluded that it was impossible for any woman, past, present, or future, to have the genius of Shakespeare. Woolf imagined that Shakespeare might have had a brilliant sister named Judith who faced impossible obstacles and that "any woman born with a great gift in the sixteenth century would certainly have gone crazed, shot herself, or ended her days in some lonely cottage outside the village, half witch, half wizard, feared and mocked at."

That night Aphra dreamt that, as the historical Aphra Behn, she wrote a play about Mary Queen of Scots, but didn't present it as her own work because it might prove politically dangerous to do so. It cast a bad light on the memory of Queen Elizabeth who was revered by all and Mary Queen of Scots who was the great-grandmother of the reigning king, Charles II. Her play was based on the premise that Elizabeth and Mary were lovers, and that Elizabeth's anger at Mary was that of a scorned and betrayed lover. In the dream, Aphra claimed that this play she had written was a manuscript she had found, a lost play by

Shakespeare, and critics seconded that attribution, praising the masculine genius that had conceived of such a story and executed it with such skill, claiming it was the best of his histories. Aphra basked in the glory of such praise.

In her next dream, Aphra was Judith, the sister of Shakespeare, who Virginia Woolf had invented. Wishing to live an independent life in an era when a woman either belonged to her parents or to her husband, Judith, with the help of Will, and for the benefit of her parents and neighbors in Stratford-on-Avon, staged a mock wedding. One of Will's actor friends pretended to marry her, passing himself off as a merchant with a residence in London who frequently travelled on the Continent on business. Will was a little-known actor and unsuccessful playwright until Judith started writing plays under his name. By day, she played the role of a respectable matron, who, in the absence of her husband, indulged her passion for theater, frequently attending productions at the Globe. By night, she would disguise herself and, following her whim, would sample multiple styles of life under multiple identities, both male and female, in everyday London and at Court. She enjoyed the praise her works engendered, as well as her secrecy, which gave her an aura of mystery and left her free to do whatever she pleased with whomever she pleased.

When Nell had her turn, she dreamt that, as in history, she was the mistress of King Charles II. But in the dream, she heightened his interest and her pleasure by role play and cross dressing. One night she would dress as a man and he as a woman. Another, she'd be a woman and he a man. And on other nights they would both be women, or both be men. They determined their gender roles for the night by cutting a deck of cards. Each would turn over one card after the other until a queen or king appeared. If a queen, he or she would be a woman, and if a king a man.

When Fanny slept on the sofa, she dreamt that in the twenty-first century, she was diagnosed with breast cancer, given the latest non-invasive treatments and completely cured. Then she woke up as Fanny Burney, AKA Madame d'Arblay and found herself naked on a butcher table. She was drunk but conscious, this being before anesthetics much less any knowledge of the dangers of infection. Scalpel in hand, a man grabbed hold of her breast then stood back in surprise, then stepped forward again and squeezed here and there on both breasts. "It's not there," he said. "The lump isn't there anymore. It's a miracle. These are miracle breasts," and he kissed them again and again, sucking hard on each nipple, and the man doing the sucking wasn't a doctor at all, it was General Alexandre d'Arblay whom she had married at the age of forty-one. He was an exiled French nobleman who had been adjutant general to Lafayette, who was a hero of both the American and French Revolutions. They made love on the table, and it was her first time, the first of many, the blood of her hymen staining the wood instead of blood from her planned mastectomy. As she woke, she was thinking of how she would describe this scene in her diary and also wondering what sex would be like when she wasn't drunk and was lying comfortably in bed. What positions they might try, what was physically possible given the limitations of human anatomy and the creativity of lascivious minds.

When it was Cat's turn again, she dreamt that as Catharine Macaulay she travelled to Vienna, ostensibly to do research for her history of England in the seventeenth century. There, at the opera house, she met the infamous Casanova. At intermission, he led her to an empty dressing room in the basement. On a sofa very much like the sofa in Dick and Belle's apartment, they made love repeatedly, and missed the rest of the opera.

In the morning, Mercy walked in wondering why Dick and Belle and Jemmie and Cat were late for breakfast, and found Cat and Jemmie, naked and entangled on the floor.

On the way to the dining room Jemmie danced and sang, "Can you dance the Casanova that we love so well?"

28 ~ Each of Us Is All of Us

Over the following days, the relationship among Jemmie and his ladies gradually morphed. At first they took turns, then they competed for who got to stay with Jemmie each night. Then all of them slept, or didn't sleep, with him every night.

Meanwhile, each day, Mercy, with the help of Abe, and always accompanied by Belle, in her wheelchair, continued Dick's music therapy in the activity room.

Once, standing by the piano at Mercy's side, Abe staggered. Mercy caught him before he could fall.

"I had a dream," he tried to explain. "But how could I have a dream when I wasn't asleep?"

"And what do you think you dreamed?" asked Mercy.

"I was riding on a broomstick. It wasn't my broomstick. It belonged to Belle, to Grace. I was sitting behind her like sitting behind someone on a motorcycle, and I was holding on tightly to her with one hand and to the stick with the other. My eyes were shut. I was afraid I would lean too far to the right or to the left and fall off or knock the broomstick off course so we'd wind up in the wrong place or at the wrong time. I was Harry Potter, having hitched a ride to Hogwarts with a witch who wouldn't explain anything to me.

"The traffic got heavy. There were people on broomsticks all around us, racing up and down, to the left and right of me, coming straight at us. A near miss knocked off my tri-cornered hat. I was dressed as I was for the masked ball. A ball, with wings, like a quidditch ball, flew straight at my head—a ball wearing a mask. Everyone was wearing masks, including me.

"We flew through the open window of a large stone building, not Hogwarts. It was a castle in Stockholm, and everyone was speaking Swedish. I was Swedish. This was a vast hall in a palace. There was a stack of pies on the main table on the stage at the front of the room. The king, in full regalia, walked up and down the main aisle, handing out pies.

"When it was my turn, the crowd applauded and chanted, 'Speech! Speech!'

"And I said, I'm sure this is what I said, 'Each of us is all of us.'"

"'Bravo, bravo,'" they called.

"And I was them, and they were me, and I was everyone who had ever been and everyone who would ever be. And I woke up here on this stage in the activity room with you and Dick and Belle, only I had never fallen asleep. And now I remember Dick talking about Swedenborg and Leibniz and the thesis he meant to write."

Dick waved his left arm in assent.

Abe continued, "And somehow I knew what Dick knew and I thought what Dick thought. And I knew that late in life, Swedenborg went through a personality change, like you said about left brain and right brain. Maybe he had a stroke. Maybe it was a long-term effect of slow breathing—deliberately restricting the flow of oxygen to his brain for daily meditation. Carbon dioxide can affect brain function and vision. In any case, he stopped his scientific work. He no longer could believe in the basic tenets of science that what can't be measured isn't real and that what isn't simple can't be true. He began conversing with angels and demons. He claimed to have mystically travelled to other planets, and he described his experiences there in detail. He believed that what we call gravitation is one fork of a mighty stream for which we have no name. Emerson said of him, 'He seemed, by the variety and amount of his powers, to be a composition of several persons.' His writings led to the founding of a new religion, an offshoot of Christianity.

"To these thoughts inspired by Swedenborg, Dick added notions borrowed from Leibniz, who believed that the microcosm, the small world of you and me, reflects the macrocosm—big world of the universe.

"Dick concluded that we all have within us the seeds of many personalities. Circumstances beyond our control determine which becomes dominant in our everyday life; but the seeds remain, enabling us to empathize with others and to enjoy fiction in all its forms, identifying with characters who seem very different from us. This is how we bridge the gap between our personal subjective world and objective reality. We enjoy role-play and acting, for the fun of pretending to be someone else, getting a sense of what it would feel like to be in their skin, to see and feel the world the way they do. Identity is fate, and we sometimes have the urge to break out of fate.

"Also, there's a connection between forgetting and transformation. As we grow older and forget more, as we find ourselves in new circumstances, spouse and friends having died or moved away, our everyday identity can weaken, and a new personality can begin to express itself.

"I think this is what Dick was getting at when he talked about how actors can play characters who are unlike them. And this is how Shakespeare was able to create many different characters who are still believable and memorable four hundred years later. And this is how we are able to enjoy plays and movies and novels, identifying with characters who seem very different from us. And this, too, is the basis of Jemmie's naming. He recognizes personalities within us that we have the potential to become; and at this stage of our lives and in this place, we are suggestible, willing to believe that Jemmie's names have special meaning. And we relish the idea of being more than one person, having more than one life, as do actors and authors and even readers. Each of us is all of us."

29 ~ The Genius of George Washington

"Clinton," Mercy shouted, waking from a dream. "Clinton. Not George, not Hillary. Henry, the British general."

"What the hell?" asked Abe, rolling over, rubbing his eyes, and getting his bearings. Yes, they were in his apartment, in his bed.

"In my dream, I was in Plymouth, reading dispatches from the Committees of Correspondence. It was the genius of Washington that struck me, how completely he had fooled Clinton in New York. Of course, what he had done in Boston six years earlier was brilliant, too, but not as decisive."

"Since when are you a history expert?"

"Since Jemmie called me Mercy and you Burgoyne. Since I've been reading Mercy's history of the Revolution. History, the way it was fed to me in school, was never interesting. But tonight, the facts that I had read became real to me in my dream, like I was there and living it. In my dream I was both reading the dispatches and writing a massive letter to my friend Cat, Catharine Macaulay in England. I would keep a copy of that letter for myself, as notes for the book I planned to write. If Cat could write history, why not I?"

"And what did Washington do in Boston that was such a big deal? I don't know much, but I do know that he arrived there after Concord and Lexington, after Bunker Hill. He had nothing to do with any of the fighting in Massachusetts."

"It was the summer of 1775, a year before the Declaration of Independence. Most members of the Continental Congress didn't want war. They were hoping and expecting that England would agree to reasonable terms. The make-shift army under Washington was a preventive measure in case the British should decide to retaliate and punish the colonists of Massachusetts for opening hostilities. Both sides were holding fire, waiting for diplomacy to resolve their differences. Washington had a small force of untrained farmers and tradesmen, facing an army of professional soldiers. There was no telling how long the negotiations between Congress in Philadelphia and the King and his Ministers in

London would drag on. It took six weeks for a message to go from one place to the other.

"When Washington arrived in Boston, he learned that his forces had just three rounds of gun powder per soldier. That deficiency was a closely held secret. If the British had known, they could have wiped out the colonists with the greatest of ease. Washington acted as if nothing were amiss. He had his troops build fortifications on the hills around Boston. He acted as if he had all the ammunition he might ever need.

"The local farmers had little gunpowder to spare. The southern colonies eventually sent some along. The locals did their best to tool up to produce gunpowder, but that took time. What made a real difference was pirates, privateers, empowered to prey on British shipping and to capture whatever military supplies they could. And in the meantime, Washington successfully carried on his charade, tricking the British into thinking that he was well supplied, and they were at risk."

"And what does that have to do with Clinton and New York?"

"Boston was the first indicator of his genius. He would have been great at poker, bluffing to get the most out of his cards, even when he had a losing hand.

"Six years later, after Burgoyne, your other self, had lost the Battle of Saratoga, and France had entered the war as an ally of the colonists, Clinton was in command of the British forces in America, with his headquarters in New York City. Washington had a small force, consisting mostly of untrained recruits. That was the norm because volunteers would come and go, heading home when they wanted to plant and harvest and take care of family matters. Now he had a small French army as well, under the Count of Rochambeau. They joined forces in White Plains, near New York City. And a French squadron had set sail from Rhode Island, presumably heading for New York as well."

"And you remember all this?"

"As if I had written it."

"As you did, of course," Abe chuckled.

"Well, Clinton intercepted dispatches from Washington confirming plans for attack, and either those dispatches were decoys, or Washington, knowing they had been intercepted, changed his plans. His army was far smaller and weaker than Clinton presumed, and news had arrived that Britain had renewed its alliance with the Emperor of Germany and the Emperor was sending more Hessian mercenaries. So instead of attacking New York City, Washington marched all the way to Virginia in three weeks. And the French squadron in Rhode Island sailed south rather than to New York and joined a French fleet that was already in the Chesapeake, bringing another 3,000 troops for Washington's army. And all that while they were heading to Virginia, a skeleton force left behind by Washington kept up the appearance that the rebels were at full strength and ready to attack New York, marching back and forth on the ramparts of forts, maybe carrying broomsticks instead of guns. Clinton was so convinced of the imminent danger that he sent orders to Cornwallis in Virginia to send some of his troops north to help defend New York when Cornwallis, in fact, was about to be attacked.

"Also, the Battle of Yorktown itself wasn't a clash of armies on an open field. Rather it was fought and won mainly by shovels. The British had just 400 shovels; the colonists had far more. The colonists dug trenches parallel to the British earthwork defenses, moved up their cannon and bombarded. Then they dug channels leading closer and dug trenches parallel again so they could move their guns up again. And so on. Meanwhile the British, who were stuck on a narrow peninsula, blocked on the land by the combined American and French armies, and on the sea by the French fleet, were running out of food and ammunition. Cornwallis tried to save the bulk of his army by sending them up the river on boats, but a storm broke that up. Despairing that his army would be totally destroyed before reinforcements arrived from Clinton in New York, Cornwallis surrendered."

"And what's so important about all that to you?"

"I'm used to thinking of history as inevitable—that what happened had to happen—it was fated. But what if nothing was fated? What if one unlikely event after another happened, like Washington having the genius or the luck to fool Clinton and march, unnoticed, all the way to Virginia. What if it was just by chance that things turned out the way they did? What if, with one small change, it could have turned out very differently? If the people involved in those events had suspected how much depended on even their smallest actions, that would be a heavy responsibility. Crippling, probably. They might be so afraid to do the wrong thing that they wouldn't do anything at all."

30 ~ Philomela and the Scarlet Letter

The next night Mercy had a very different dream.

"Johnny, I'm ashamed. I dreamt a story that's deeply disturbing and that I'm ashamed of."

"How can you be ashamed of a dream?"

"I believe that the dreams we've shared these last few weeks are real. And I believe what I just saw in this dream actually did happen or could have happened. If it didn't happen that was just a matter of chance, because I wanted it to happen. It was in me to be that unfaithful, that wicked. That was me. I was responsible for it."

"So, this is you as Mercy Warren, at the time of the Revolution, not you in your present life?"

"Of course."

"Then it can't possibly be true, and you have no reason to feel ashamed even if you are in some sense that woman as well as the woman you are now. I read the same biography of her that you did, and I'm convinced that Mercy Warren would never do anything shameful. She was a saint, a Puritan saint. Her one and only love was the man she married. That's what everyone who knew her believed. And the many letters she exchanged with friends leave no doubt about that."

"You forget Philomela."

"And who is Philomela?"

"For many years, that's how Mercy signed the letters she wrote to Abigail Adams and other intimate friends. Philomela."

"And what does that mean?"

"Philomela was a character in Ovid's *Metamorphoses*. She was raped by her brother-in-law, who cut out her tongue so she couldn't accuse him, and the gods turned her into a nightingale."

"How thoughtful of the gods. What a fitting compensation for what she went through. And why the hell would Mercy Warren have chosen a character like that as her alter ego?"

"The brother-in-law."

"Did Mercy have a brother-in-law?"

"No. As far as I can tell, she didn't. But she had the next best thing."

"And what is the next best thing to a brother-in-law?"

"Joseph Warren. He wasn't related to my husband James Warren, at least not closely— maybe distant cousins. But Joseph was a good friend and a close associate in the rebel cause. He was a widower, having married an heiress who died soon after. In those days it was common for women to die young, especially in childbirth. Joseph visited often at Mercy's house in Plymouth. He was a physician and also the President of the Massachusetts Provincial Congress. And after Joseph was killed at the Battle of Bunker Hill, James replaced him as President. Some people mistakenly thought that they were brothers."

"So, you think he raped her?"

"I think either she wished he had, or that they were lovers, when James was away, which was often."

"That seems far-fetched."

"It isn't a matter of evidence. I feel it in my bones, which are her bones. I feel the shame, as if I were Hester Prynne wearing a scarlet letter for everyone to see."

"The Hawthorne overtones of this place are getting to you."

"When I dreamt it last night, it was as real as anything that happened to me here today or yesterday. The story involves an old friend of yours."

"You mean a friend of Burgoyne?"

"Of course. General Thomas Gage. You were friends in school, at the Westminster School, at Westminster Abbey. Remember that dream you had about leaving for school for the first time at the age of ten? Gage was stationed in the colonies during the French and Indian War. He went on Braddock's disastrous expedition, along with George Washington. He and Washington were friends. Three years later he married Margaret Kemble of New Jersey.

"In 1774, Gage was appointed military governor of Massachusetts. He withdrew the British garrisons from New York City, New Jersey, Philadelphia, Halifax and Newfoundland and brought them all to Boston. Then reinforcements arrived, doubling the number of British regulars in his command and bringing three more generals — William Howe, Henry Clinton, and you -- John Burgoyne."

"This sounds more like a history lesson than a dream."

"I'll get to the dream. But to make sense of the dream, you need to understand the context, which was on my mind from having read up on the Revolution in the library, after last night's dream about Washington.

"Gage's wife, Margaret, was with him in Boston. And the war had not yet started. People we remember as patriots moved freely in and out of Boston. Prominent colonists socialized with British officers and their wives. In addition to his roles as physician and as President of the Massachusetts Provincial Congress, Joseph Warren was a major general in the Massachusetts militia. The size of the militia and the location of its stores of guns and ammunition were secrets, but the British had spies everywhere. Many colonists were loyal to England and were more than willing to help king and country with tidbits of information. Gage knew who the leaders of the resistance were. He went by the adage: keep your friends close and your enemies closer. Right up until the outbreak of hostilities, he welcomed to his house Joseph Warren and others who we now think of as patriots. That was a way to lull the would-be rebels into a false sense of security.

"But Gage's pretty wife was herself a colonist and felt conflicted being married to the commander of the British forces. And Joseph Warren went out of his way to cultivate her as a source of information, and as a lover. They had what could be called a patriotic affair, an affair to be remembered. When Margaret learned that Gage planned to seize Sam Adams and John Hancock in Lexington and then to burn the military supplies stored in Concord, she alerted Joseph Warren. He spread the word by way of Paul Revere, William Dawes, and Samuel Prescott, and hence the Minutemen were ready at Lexington and Concord. Gage had only shared that plan with one person—Margaret. She was clearly the source of the leak. He shipped her back to England immediately."

"And what does that have to do with Mercy and your dream?"

"In the first part of my dream, Joseph bragged about his conquest, not military, sexual. James, Joseph, and I were eating a turkey dinner at our house in Plymouth. 'I'm a free agent,' he insisted. 'A widower. A bachelor, with no romantic ties. Seducing Margaret, I wasn't being unfaithful to anyone. Rather, I was cuckolding the British military governor, a patriotic act and a pleasurable one as well. She's a joy to behold and to hold.'

"James congratulated Joseph, finding it amazing that he was capable of such duplicity, which seemed so counter to his character, but which was essential for the cause of rebellion. But the moral ambiguity of the situation made him feel uncomfortable. James himself would never be able to do such a thing. The end doesn't justify the means.

"'Nonsense,' Joseph persisted. 'Remember the example of Judith in the Book of Judges. She seduced Holofernes, the commander of the Babylonian army. And when he was asleep, she chopped off his head. For that, she's deemed a heroine, a patriot. I, too, seduced an enemy for the good of the cause. But I didn't chop her head off. I just took information. I'm sure that the general was furious when he figured out what had happened. But his wife was none the worse for it. I wasn't her first, nor will she be my last, God willing. In fact, I'm sure she was well pleased, and better pleased than she had been in many a year.'

"'You seem quite pleased with yourself,' I ventured.

"Joseph winked and smiled. Maybe he was putting on this uncharacteristic display of braggadocio to deflect suspicion from the two of us. Maybe this was his way of protecting and honoring me. But it stung. And with James in the house, I wouldn't be able to talk to Joseph intimately and find out what he really meant. I didn't know if I could ever trust and believe him again, now that I had seen this other side of him, this other person he could be. I felt betrayed. But in betraying me and using Margaret, if, in fact, he felt no love for her, he was saving the Revolution. Without that warning, the rebellion would have ended right there.

"Then my dream jumped forward to when I learned the outcome of the Battle of Bunker Hill. After the battles of Lexington and Concord, General Gage and his troops were bottled up in Boston. The narrow strip of land connecting the city with the mainland was blockaded by rebel troops. To break the blockade, Gage sent a couple thousand soldiers across the harbor to Charleston where they fought the Battle of Bunker Hill. Technically that was a British victory, but more than half the British troops were killed or wounded. The rebels took heart— outnumbered, poorly armed, untrained, and undisciplined, they had held off a far superior professional army. Yes, they retreated, but the war had just begun, and they would fight another day.

"Joseph Warren, who had no military experience, was the general in charge of the rebel army that day. James Warren was also there.

"During the retreat, Joseph was shot in the head. He died immediately. That's where the rest of my dream began.

"A rider brought news of the battle to Plymouth. The war had begun in earnest, and the rebels had held their own. General Warren was dead, but the British had suffered heavy casualties, and the Americans had retreated intact."

"Hearing that General Warren was dead, I first thought that meant my husband James. I was shaken with conflicting feelings, covering my face and running back into my house—not wanting others to guess what I was thinking before I knew what I was thinking myself. I had lost my husband, who I loved. But now I was free to be with Joseph, whom I also loved, with a passion, a sinful passion, unlike my sisterly devotion to James.

"Then a neighbor rushed into the house, concerned that I might have misheard and could be devastated by the misunderstanding. It was Joseph Warren who had died, not James.

"Hearing that, I collapsed and convulsed in sobs. Joseph was dead and James was saved, and I was wracked with guilt and shame that so much of me wished it was the other way around."

31 ~ The Mistress of Bath

"I, too, had a dream of shame, but mine was far worse than yours," Abe told her. "You remember that I or rather Burgoyne was the one who came up with the plan that led to the Battle of Saratoga. I was to march south from Canada, and General Howe was to march north to meet me. Lord Germain never sent the orders to Howe, so I walked into a trap and my entire army was captured.

"In my dream, I left Lord Germain abruptly, not waiting to make sure he transmitted the orders to Howe. I told him that I needed to return to my wife, Charlotte, who was deathly ill. But, instead, I was in a hurry to get to Bath, even though my wife was ill in London, far more ill than I imagined.

"Susan Caulfield, the actress and opera singer, my new-found mistress, was waiting for me in Bath, and I would be gone for a year or more. I was anxious to spend as much time with her as I could before leaving—making memories to last the long absence.

"Charlotte, the lady I eloped with in that dream you and I shared, died while I was in America, losing the Battle of Saratoga and the war as well.

"When I returned to London, paroled after having been captured at Saratoga, I became a playwright, and Susan moved in with me, and we lived as husband and wife, though we never married. We had four children together."

"You bastard!"

"Yes, I probably was. Rumor had it that my god father, Lord Bingley, was my earthly father as well."

"I don't mean your blood. I mean your soul. How could you do that? Run off for a trysting holiday with your mistress while your wife was dying, and your army and your country were depending on you to deal seriously with the business of war?"

"But if I had been morally upright and had made sure about the orders, England would have won the war and America would never have won its independence. Unintended consequences. My moral failure, my shame won the revolution for you."

"You are totally revolting."

"Not me. Not this me. That other me."

"That's so typical of you. Not taking responsibility for your actions, your sins, your mortal sins."

"Now you're sounding like that other Mercy. But remember, as you just told me, she, too, had her guilt and her shame. I thought that Charlotte was feigning her illness. She knew about Susan, though we never talked about that. She never confronted me about it, but she must have heard or figured it out. I thought she was jealous and trying to get back at me by keeping me home when she knew I was itching to be with her rival. The more she told me of her symptoms, the more I believed it was a farce, that she was acting even better than her actress competitor. I would have none of that. But I was wrong. Dead wrong. She died.

"When I headed to Bath, I didn't care about scandal. Affairs and mistresses were commonplace. I had to be careful as long as Charlotte's father the Earl of Derby was alive. My career and my fortune depended on him. But he had died a few months before, so I was liberated from his constraining influence. I was finally free to openly enjoy my love, my Susan."

"Well at least you were loyal to your mistress."

"After a fashion."

"What?"

"At least as long as I lived."

"Meaning what?"

"I left her out of my will. I left her nothing. And in my will, I stipulated that our children be taken away from her to be raised by my relatives."

"Unspeakable!"

"Mea culpa. I've regretted that since the day I died."

32 ~ A Campfire in Portugal

The next night Abe had two dreams, both historical, and both starting from the same scene. He looked up the background in the library before he told the story to Mercy and the rest of the group that evening at dinner. They were all assembled and all of them dressed in their masquerade attire.

"One dream was based on history, and the other was not," Abe explained. "Both dreams started around a campfire in Portugal. I was Burgoyne, a general, in command of a joint Portuguese-British force, preparing to attack the Spanish and French who were poised to invade Portugal. The afternoon before the surprise attack I had planned for that night, I was playing the card game Ombre with the traditional 40-card deck. My opponent was Charles Lee, a lieutenant colonel of cavalry who was to lead the charge that night. Of course, I had no idea at the time that this Lee would become a general fighting for the colonists in the Revolutionary War. I had no idea there would ever be such a war. And this was not Lighthorse Harry Lee, the revolutionary hero who was the father of Robert E. Lee. Rather, this was Charles Lee who later sought the job of commander-in-chief of the Continental Army, but instead became Washington's second-in-command. The Charles Lee who was court-martialed after he ordered a retreat when the rest of the army was attacking at the Battle of Monmouth, and who later turned out to have been a traitor, not just a fool.

"Here, more than a decade before all that, I made the mistake of playing cards with Charles Lee.

"This Lee had experience in combat from the French and Indian War a few years before. He had been on Braddock's March with George Washington and with Tom Gage, who later commanded the British in Boston, the Gage whose wife betrayed him to Joseph Warren.

"While in America, Lee had married the daughter of a Mohawk chief and had twins with her. The Mohawks called him 'Boiling Water.' He often told that story, proud of that name, which should have been a clue that he had a hot temper and wasn't ashamed of it, wasn't ashamed of anything.

"Before this campfire card game, I had only known Lee by his military record. He had fought at Louisburg, Fort Ticonderoga, Fort Niagara, and Montreal before coming to Portugal. Those were impressive credentials. But I was aloof, kept to myself, and only fraternized with a few officers who I knew well and trusted. I made an exception this time, having given this man a dangerous assignment—a surprise attack at night with a hundred cavalrymen against a much larger force. The plan was good. The odds of success were great. But it felt right to share a bottle of scotch and play a game of Ombre with the man I had chosen to execute it.

"On paper, Lee was a gentleman—the son of a general, he owned extensive estates in England. But he acted like a rowdy infantry sergeant, not a cavalry colonel. Seeing him up close, and spending a couple hours with him, I never wanted to see the man again. He was eccentric and slovenly in appearance and coarse in language. His grooming was unbecoming an officer, and his manners, well, he had no manners. This was not the kind of man I would choose to associate with. I would be ashamed to be seen with him in London. And that was before I caught him cheating at cards over a bet of five shillings. I didn't say a word. It wasn't worth exchanging insults over such a petty sum. I don't play cards with cheats, and I would have nothing to do with him again.

"As expected, the attack worked, and we retook the village of Vita Velha. Also, as expected, Lee bragged loudly about his own bravery, as if the success had all been due to him. For the follow-up action on the Tagus River, which decisively ended the war in that sector, I didn't use him at all, didn't want him. I never spoke another word to him.

"I learned from research that after Portugal, Lee served as aide-de-camp under King Stanislaw II of Poland. He fought in the Russo-Turkish War. He lost two fingers in a duel in which he killed his opponent. And when tensions started to rise between England and the American colonies, he returned to America in anticipation that war might break out. He bought a large estate in what is now West Virginia, near the home of his friend Horatio Gates, a retired British officer who later as a rebel general would defeat me, Burgoyne, at the Battle of Saratoga. Then he travelled through the colonies for nearly a year, making friends among those who favored a break with England. When hostilities broke out, he resigned his British commission and volunteered for the Continental Army, hoping and expecting to be named commander-in-chief, because of the friends he had made and because he was by far the most experienced candidate. But in his appearance before the Continental Congress, he was as slovenly and ill-mannered as he had been with me in Portugal. He made much of the fact that by joining the rebellion, he forfeited all his properties in England, and he wanted Congress to compensate him for that. So, they passed him over and chose Washington instead. He served under Washington, as his second-in-command, but continued to politic against him, trying to get his job. He was captured in New Jersey and released a year and a half later in a prisoner exchange. His retreat at the Battle of Monmouth cost that battle, and he was suspended for incompetence. But documents uncovered long after his death showed that while a prisoner of the British, he had drafted a plan for British operations against the Americans.

"That's the way it turned out in history. But in my second dream, due to a slight change, history went in a different direction. In that dream, other matters came up and I didn't show for the card game. Lee drank alone, and I never got to know him, never found out he was a card cheat, and hence just thought of him as a fellow British officer who had served under me in Portugal.

"In that dream, Lee, after he had established himself in America, invited me to join the rebel cause. He knew that I had spoken in Parliament in favor of the colonists. He believed that war was imminent. He imagined himself as commander-in-chief and me as his second-in-command.

"I answered the call and went with Lee to the Continental Congress when he sought the position of commander. But while Lee was arrogant, slovenly, and disrespectful, I was true to my nickname, a gentleman with the bearing, the look, the temperament, the manner of a general, and experience as a general as well. Congress picked me instead of Lee and instead of Washington.

"I marched on New York immediately and rather than attack, I made generous offers of land to deserters. I was familiar with recruiting practices in England. Many of those soldiers had been tricked into enlisting or had joined up out of poverty and desperation. And the Hessians were no better than slaves to their royal master who was paid by the British for their services. When it became clear that desertion was safe and the rewards were real, the British army dissolved without firing a shot.

"Soon thereafter, France joined the side of the colonists and England sought peace. In the treaty, Canada was returned to France as a reward for their help. I settled in New York where I became a playwright."

"And did we meet?" asked Mercy. "Did I move to New York and become a playwright as well, and did we live happily ever after?"

"Of course," he said with a smile, but she didn't believe him.

33 ~ Senator Warren from Massachusetts

"This must be contagious," said Cat. "I, too, had an historical dream, nearly as wild and improbable as yours, Johnny. Over the last couple weeks, I've read all three volumes of Mercy's history and all eight volumes of Macaulay's. The reading was easy and fast as if I was already familiar with those books.

"Catherine Macaulay, my other self according to Jemmie, the first British woman historian, corresponded with Mercy Warren for many years and visited America after the Revolution. She spent a month with Mercy, then went to New York, Philadelphia, and Virginia to meet and interview major figures in the Revolution for a projected history, which she never got around to writing, due to illness. Mercy was also writing a history of the Revolution, but she was slow about it, interrupted by family crises, and didn't publish it until 1805, after John Marshall's *Life of George Washington* had appeared and been recognized as the standard work on the subject.

"In my dream, I, Catherine Macaulay, rather than return to England, stayed in America, encouraged Mercy to write her history and helped her with it. It was published in 1786, instead of 1805, long before Marshall's book. Because of the timing, Mercy's book got wide-spread recognition.

"Then, thanks to my prompting and with the help of members of the Massachusetts Legislature who knew and respected both Mercy and her husband, Mercy was named to the Constitutional Convention. I went to Philadelphia with her. There she fought hard but unsuccessfully to give women the right to vote. She couldn't even win a compromise to let women have half a vote.

"Instead, in both history and in my dream, the Constitution granted to the states the power to set voting requirements. In Massachusetts, you had to be a man over the age of twenty-one and have been a resident for a year preceding, with an annual income of three pounds or with an estate of worth sixty pounds.

"There was never anything in the Constitution to prevent women from running for office and serving in Congress or even as President.

The writers of the Constitution never imagined such an eventuality, so they didn't explicitly prohibit it. The text specifying the qualifications for office used the word 'person', not man. *No Person except a natural born Citizen ... shall be eligible to the Office of President ...*

"In my dream, Mercy was aware of that loophole and therefore didn't bring up that issue for debate. She was then selected by the Massachusetts state legislature as one of the first two senators from Massachusetts. She would never have been elected by the populace at large, but she had many friends in the legislature.

"She was reelected to the Senate repeatedly, and Jefferson selected her as his running mate in 1804, to balance the ticket North/South, instead of George Clinton of New York, who was his choice historically.

"Then, in 1808, she was elected President, the first woman president. She was re-elected in 1812 and died in October 1814, to be succeeded by her vice president, James Madison. Always a foe of England during her tenure in office, she built up the Army and the Navy and the defenses around Washington DC, in anticipation of a British invasion. So, when the British attacked in August 1814, they were repulsed, and the White House and Capitol were never burned."

34 ~ Journey of Discovery

One night, when Abe handed out wine bottles at dinner, he noted, "We won't be able to indulge like this much longer. The wine attic is nearly empty."

Dick waved his left hand to get attention, then wrote, "Cellar, try cellar."

"Is there a cellar?" asked Abe.

And Jemmie chanted, "Wine cellar, wine cellar, sell me some wine."

Abe asked at the front desk, "Is there a cellar?"

"Yes, but it's unheated and there are no lights. There's no electricity at all. It's full of trash, and the wooden stairs down to it are rotten. No one has been down there in decades. We keep it locked for the safety of the residents."

Back at the dinner table, Abe reported, "No luck there, unless one of you knows how to pick locks."

Mercy smiled, "Back in college, a friend of mine would shop-lift one day and shop-return the next for the thrill of it. And her boyfriend, Jason, burgled for fun. He would break into a house and take random stuff, then break in again a week later and return it. The local paper reported the incidents humorously as poltergeist activity. The police stopped investigating saying it was a waste of their time. Well, Jason taught me how to pick locks. Padlocks are easy. All it takes is a hairpin."

Abe got his flashlight. Mercy picked the lock. Then they slowly, carefully descended into the depths.

Cold, no heat, just the warmth that came through the poorly insulated floor above. It had a dirt floor. Ice in a winding trail. Probably, a tiny stream meandered through there in the summer.

Broken furniture and other trash were stacked up to the ceiling. When they cleared a narrow path through it, they saw what looked like the bottom of a door.

They cleared the way to the door and opened it into a room with row upon row of wooden shelving, each shelf stacked with jars of fruits and vegetables, probably the result of home canning a hundred years or more ago. The stench was overpowering. They backed out into the first room to catch their breath and cover their mouths with handkerchiefs. Then they plunged back in.

They tried to squeeze past the first rack of shelves. It tipped and fell with a crash. Jars broke, spilling their putrid contents on the dirt floor. They tried to squeeze past the next one, and that one fell into the next and that the next. Beyond the debris, they saw other shelves built into the stone wall that was probably the foundation of the building. These shelves extended for a hundred feet or more, half a foot between shelves, a dozen shelves from floor to ceiling, and bottles of wine, on their side, packed tight on every shelf.

They walked the length of this treasure trove, Abe waving the beam of the flashlight up, down, and around, in delight. The bottles resembled the ones in the attic. Perhaps this wine, too, was still good for drinking.

Then Mercy called from the far side of the room. "There's another door back here."

"Well open it, for God's sake. We can't stay down here forever, not without a gas mask."

"There's a tunnel."

"A what?"

"A tunnel. It's dark in there. I can't tell how far it goes."

Abe handed her the flashlight, and she led the way.

The entrance was only four feet high, and just wide enough for one person to walk through without having to turn sideways. The tunnel itself was just as low and narrow. Walking, bent over, was difficult.

The tunnel wound. They went ten steps forward then had to turn sharply to the right, then to the left, then to the right again, at odd angles. Then the tunnel forked in three directions. When Mercy chose the far left, without hesitation, Abe reached out and stopped her.

"We have to be sure we can find our way back."

"Okay, Hansel. Did you bring breadcrumbs?"

"Seriously. There are lots of loose rocks along our path. Whenever we have to make a choice of direction, we should mark where we came from by forming an arrow with rocks."

They sat on the cold ground and made their first arrow. They needed a break. It was exhausting walking bent over.

They continued and a door appeared on the left, then another on the right, right again, then left, left, left. Then Mercy stopped abruptly. She felt drawn to this door. She and Abe made another arrow, then Mercy pulled on the latch.

The door opened half-way, just wide enough for them to squeeze through.

Finally, they could stand up straight. They were in a basement, but it felt like they were in a different basement. The walls were brick, not stone. Barrels and wooden crates were stacked neatly along the walls, and, at the far end, there was a brick staircase.

They could hear footsteps above them, many footsteps.

With all the twists and turns of the tunnel, it was difficult to say how far they had gone. But they had been walking for over two hours. Even at their slow pace, they must have covered at least a mile, probably more. And the buildings of Arcadia Estates only extended for a quarter mile, at most, in any direction. There was no other dwelling on this side of the mountain.

They slowly and cautiously climbed the stairs, then opened the door at the top. They found themselves in a tavern packed with customers, all of whom were dressed as they were. A door on the far side of this new room swung open revealing a large meeting hall.

"Faneuil Hall," Mercy whispered to Abe. "I've been here before, in Boston, only that was more than two hundred years in the future."

"Free beer for all," shouted a waiter, handing a tankard to Mercy and another to Abe. "This is a day to remember."

"And what day is that?" asked Abe.

"Why election day of course."

Mercy declined politely. Abe took a tankard without thinking and drank quickly, spilling beer on his waistcoat and britches. The beer was cold, refreshing, and much needed after their long trek through the low and narrow tunnel.

Mercy pulled him close and whispered, "We have to get out of here. Fast. Now!"

35 ~ Risks and Plans

"Why the panic?" Abe yelled as they rushed back through the tunnel.

"This is real," she screamed.

As they passed through the wine cellar, Abe grabbed an armful of wine. Mercy couldn't care less—she wanted to get out as soon as possible.

She alerted the others. And when they had all assembled in the activity room, Mercy told them, "You're all here. Arcadia is here. Everything is as it was. That's good. That's great. That's incredible."

"What are you talking about?" asked Cat.

"You see that wet spot on Abe's waistcoat and britches? That's beer. That's beer that was spilled on him in a tavern in Boston in 1769, less than an hour ago."

"And what is the meaning of that bizarre sentence?" Cat pursued.

"We walked into the past."

"And then ran out of it," Abe added. "Where did you get the 1769?"

"I saw the date on a newspaper in the tavern. September 5. The day James Otis got his head bashed in."

"Weird," responded Cat.

"Is that all you can say? We could have destroyed the world as we know it, and we could have destroyed that other world, too, in more ways than one. It was totally irresponsible of us to go there."

"As if we knew where we were going," added Abe.

"Can someone please unpack this conversation?" pleaded Aphra.

"This wasn't a dream," explained Mercy. "We weren't observers from afar. We were in the midst of a crowd in a tavern. They touched us. We touched them. We couldn't help it. Everyone was packed tight. Abe took hold of a tankard of beer and drank from it and spilled beer from it. What we saw was real. We were in the past and could change the past, with unintended and ever-expanding consequences. We could have erased the present that we know, even erased our own existence. We could have shifted all of history to a different track."

"Like some hoaky time-travel movie?" asked Fanny.

"Yes," admitted Mercy. "By chance, our dress was appropriate for the time. We didn't stand out, and we got out of there quickly. It looks like we lucked out on that account. But the germs still worry me."

"You mean us taking germs from our time back to their time when no one would have immunity for them?" asked Abe.

"We seem to have lucked out on that as well, since I see no sign that anything has changed in this world. But we still have to worry about the vice versa. We shouldn't be sitting here together. I should know better. Remember, I'm a nurse. Abe and I should have immediately washed ourselves and our clothes, over and over again, like astronauts returning from space. We have to hope that in our brief time there we didn't pick up microorganisms, on our clothes or on our bodies, that could contaminate people here and even spread to everywhere on Earth."

Cat interrupted, "You mean that, for however short a time it was, you actually saw, you actually lived in the past, a past from over two hundred and fifty years ago? God! What I would give to have an opportunity to do that."

"And me as well," echoed Fanny, Nell, and Aphra. And Dick waved his left hand frantically.

"No way," insisted Mercy. "I haven't a clue how that happened and whether it could happen again. But the door to the cellar should be sealed permanently. We can't risk catastrophic consequences for the sake of idle curiosity."

"It's as if we were meant to do this," Cat countered. "We don't have a choice."

"But we do have a choice. We must not go back there."

No," Cat persisted. "Think about it. These dreams we've all been having were a dress rehearsal. The names Jemmie gave us. The clothes we're wearing now. The research we were prompted to do. We've been in training for this. We're meant to do it."

"You mean meant by fate? Nonsense. There's no such thing as fate."

Dick held up his pad of paper and waved it wildly, with the word "ME" in large letters.

"No. Absolutely no, Dick. We couldn't carry you down those stairs and through that tunnel. And your wheelchair wouldn't fit in the tunnel. And what would those people think of your wheelchair?"

"But say we are meant to have seen this, to have done this" Abe speculated. "And what about the others here, the rest of the group. This isn't just about us. They've had dreams, too. And they have the clothes. They've done research. Maybe they're supposed to go as well."

"Nonsense," Mercy stood and glared at them all.

"Let's put it to a vote," suggested Cat.

Everyone but Mercy and Belle, who was in a world of her own, raised a hand.

"I can't let you do this," Mercy repeated.

"Well," Abe asked, "how could we minimize the risk of spreading disease and yet do what we are somehow meant to do? Your being a nurse and knowing about such matters might be part of fate as well. At this point I'm willing to believe anything," he added, taking out a handkerchief and rubbing the wet spots on his waistcoat and britches.

"The more people go back and forth, and the more often they do it, the greater the risk. Anyone foolish enough to go there needs to be thoroughly scrubbed and sprayed with bleach. And the clothes need to be washed in bleach as well."

"Why bleach?" asked Abe.

"That's the most effective disinfectant, and we can get it easily here."

"Check."

"And shots—every available vaccine, even though the pathogens back then would be very different from the pathogens today, it wouldn't hurt to get shots, especially for smallpox, which was common then."

"Double check. You can do that. You're recognized as a nurse here. You have access to medical supplies."

"And there is no need to go running up and down the hall opening doors. We should restrain our curiosity to minimize the risk. We should only open one more door to determine if they all might open on the same place and time."

"But," Abe objected, "we passed dozens of doors, and we have no idea how many doors there are beyond the one we opened and down other branching corridors. There could be an infinity of doors, each posing a different set of challenges and opportunities which we're meant to deal with."

"Stop saying *meant*. That's absurd. That's an excuse."

"But we would only need to open one more door to know if they all could be the same," claimed Mercy.

"And if what we saw required immediate action?"

"No way. I refuse to take part."

"Then I'll go alone," Abe insisted.

"You would do that? You would defy me on a matter of this importance? You would doubt the wisdom of my informed advice? You would go against me like that? I thought we had something special, something lasting."

"And we do. And it's wonderful. But it's tied up with this same inexplicable set of occurrences. Having the same dreams, having dreams set in the era of that other-timely world we just caught a glimpse of. That's not chance. Our having met one another here and connected so quickly and so completely ... that was meant to be. I'm sure of it. And I'm just as sure that the two of us together are meant to take the next step."

"Then we only open one door. We peek through the door. We don't even open it wide. Then we leave; we run for it."

"So, you agree we have to do this?"

"What Mercy thinks isn't the end of the matter," insisted Cat. "If we're meant to do this, if we have unwittingly been preparing for it, that's because there's something we need to change."

"And what do you think needs changing?" Abe pursued. "What mistake that humanity made would you want to reverse if you could?"

"Nonsense," insisted Mercy. "If we are to do this, it must be on the smallest possible scale, going out of our way not to change anything."

"Not do a thing, when you could better the lot of man for all time?" asked Cat. "That's scandalous."

"And what's your passion?" asked Abe again. "If you could, what would you change?"

"England. The England that Catherine Macaulay loved. The controversy over America and the rights of citizens and the rights of man and woman could lead to a democratic revolt in England. If I had a chance, I would do everything I could to make England a republic. The sooner the better."

"But maybe there are different planes of reality or parallel worlds," objected Mercy.

"If that were the case, then we wouldn't be risking our world, but we could make another world far better. We'll never know if we don't try."

"But you could end up changing everything everywhere, in ways you can't foresee. Would you be willing to accept the unintended consequences?"

"To make England a republic? Of course I would."

"Even if that meant there'd be no American Revolution? No United States of America?"

"Maybe there'd be no need for one. And no need for the Civil War, either. America could be a self-governing part of the United Republics of Great Britain, with no slavery, and with equal rights for women, and for all, regardless of their race or culture or lifestyle."

"And you'd be willing to sacrifice yourself and us and our entire world for that pipe-dream of yours?"

"Whatever it is that made possible that journey of yours has plans for us. And it's our job to figure out what we are meant to do and then to do it."

"I don't believe in mystical forces."

"And yet you believe in time travel."

"All I did was walk down a tunnel and open a door."

"And that was all it took. Let me go, and I'll make something of that opportunity, something grand and earth-shaking—perhaps leading to paradise on Earth."

"Peace on Earth, good will to men," chanted Jemmie.

"Enough," insisted Abe. "Mercy and I will go back. We'll take all the precautions, and we'll only open one door. One step at a time. One small step."

"One small step for man," intoned Jemmie.

36 ~ To Saratoga or Not to Saratoga

When they came to the door they had gone through before, Mercy wrote on the door with a felt tip pen: "Faneuil Hall, Boston, September 5, 1769."

Then they walked past many other doors without trying them. Abe was leading the way. They were here on his insistence, and he would make the choice, as she had the time before.

He hurried along, impatient, and scared of what might happen next, with no criterion in mind for how to choose the door to enter. Then he stopped short like a bull that someone had lassoed in a rodeo, and turned back to a door on the right, ten feet behind him.

He marked the door with a big X, grabbed the latch and pulled. It was stuck. He pulled with all his weight, and still it wouldn't budge. Then Mercy pulled with him, and it opened partway—far enough for one of them to squeeze through sideways.

Mercy held him back, reluctant to speak out loud, not knowing what and who might be on the other side of that door, and what response a voice from here might trigger.

Abe understood from what she had said before that she wanted him to look but not cross the threshold.

But before he could look, they were both hit first with the smells and then with the sounds. Artificial odors, probably from cologne and perfume and wig powder, overlaid on the odor of dozens or even hundreds of people who hadn't bathed in a week or a month or even longer. And the sounds of dozens or hundreds of people shuffling by, rapidly, wearing boots.

Abe turned off the flashlight and handed it to Mercy. Then he looked through the opening.

"Good God," Abe whispered urgently to Mercy. "I know this building. I've seen it in recurrent dreams about Burgoyne, in which I was Burgoyne. This is the main entrance to the Palace of Whitehall. I read about it in my research. It's a massive building, the headquarters for many government agencies. At its peak in the days of Charles II, it had over 2400 rooms and was the largest and most complex building in the western world. After fires and after some parts were torn down, it was still immense in the time of Burgoyne. In my dream, this was the building where Burgoyne met with Lord Germain, the Secretary of State for America, on that fateful day that led to disaster at Saratoga.

"There's Burgoyne himself standing on the marble staircase. I recognize him from the portrait by Reynolds. Burgoyne is standing stock-still while others rush by him, about their business. In the dream, Burgoyne's mind, my mind was blank, totally blank at this moment. I could turn around, go back up those stairs and make sure Lord Germain posted the orders to Howe, staying with him however long it took that absent-minded procrastinating bureaucrat to finish the job. I also could hurry home to my wife who might be seriously sick and not just faking it to keep me away from my rendezvous with my mistress. Or, I could rush to Bath to my mistress. Everything hinged on this moment—the Battle of Saratoga, the independence of the colonies, the entire future of the United States and the world. In my dream, Burgoyne wasn't thinking. It was as if his rational function, the left side of his brain was turned off. He was waiting for a signal from his instincts, his intuition, a gut feel, an impulse to act. The slightest disturbance, an unexpected interruption at this point could trigger a decision. I believe that if I were to call out to him now from the doorway, without even crossing the threshold, that might be enough to tip the scale and the future be changed, perhaps massively.

"I sense the guilt and shame welling up in him and the realization that Germain might forget to send the orders, and that his wife, Charlotte, might be seriously ill. I feel that guilt welling up in me as well, in sync with him. I have to—"

Mercy took hold of the flashlight with both hands and bashed him over the head with it. He fell back. She caught him. She pushed the door shut. They were in darkness. She had dropped the flashlight. She groped for it with one hand while with the other she cradled his head. When she found the flashlight and turned it on, he was conscious but confused. Thank God she hadn't killed him. She lowered him to the ground and hugged him and kissed the wound.

"I had to," she explained. "I love you, but I had to stop you. I couldn't let you change all of history just to erase the personal guilt and shame of Burgoyne. If we, all of us, are meant to do something, to change something, surely, it's not that. Let's get out of here quickly before you decide to try again and before I let you. Let's go back and scrub and wash with bleach and try to forget this whole mind-boggling corridor of alternate worlds."

"Are they worlds?" Abe mumbled in reply. "Are they real? I'm sorry. If it weren't for you, I would have called out. It was such a temptation to erase that shameful moment in Burgoyne's life, in my life. I would do anything to change that."

"And I would do anything to prevent you from intervening. That's not an acceptable risk. You would erase your guilt as Burgoyne. And you would feel you had done the honorable thing, as if you were meant to undo his sins. But the whole string of events that followed from that moment would have changed."

She kissed the wound again, and they headed back. This time they both took as many bottles of wine as they could carry.

37 ~ Mercy's Plays

When the group was gathered again in the activity room, Cat observed, "So the first two doors took you to the same time period but to different sides of the Atlantic. Mercy said she doesn't know why she picked the door she did. And you, Abe, felt like you had been lassoed and pulled back to yours. I believe that something drove you both to those specific doors."

"Something? What the hell do you mean by something?" Abe objected. "I shouldn't have said that about being lassoed. Now you're going all mystical on us."

"Admittedly, I have my passions like support for democratic practices and human rights. But I'm a practical, fact-based person. I'm not inclined toward supernatural explanations. Nonetheless, given what we've all experienced over the last few weeks and what you and Mercy encountered in the cellar, I believe that there is some intelligence that is controlling us and has been from at least when Jemmie began to name us. We are meant to do something, and we still haven't done it. There's no way we can stop here and now. I volunteer for the next trip with or without the two of you."

"When your aim is to change everything? No way," insisted Mercy.

"Then you want to do it again and with me?" Abe asked her.

"Well, I certainly don't want you to do it alone. Not with your impulses. You need a restraint, and I'm that restraint. I seem to be the only one here with a sense of responsibility."

This time, Abe carried the flashlight and led the way.

They passed the door with the big X that led to the Palace of Whitehall, and Abe felt tempted by a door fifty yards ahead on the left, but Mercy suddenly felt an uncontrollable urge, pushed her way past Abe in the narrow passageway, and opened another door on the right. She not only opened the door, she walked through. Abe followed her.

"What ...?" he started to ask, but she silenced him with her hand. People were rushing to and fro down a hallway with many doors on either side. Those people were in costume, not just the dress of the day, eighteenth-century dress, but elaborately done up and wearing heavy make-up as for a play. Masks, like the ones they had used for their masked ball, were stacked on a nearby table. Mercy took one and put it on and handed another to Abe. Then Abe had a click of recognition, took Mercy's hand, and led her down the hall to the right, then up the stairs.

"Do you know what you're doing?" whispered Mercy, when they reached the top of the stairs, among miscellaneous theatrical props.

"I've been here before. I'm sure I have. This is the Royal Theater in Drury Lane, the theater where Burgoyne's plays were performed."

The lights dimmed. An orchestra began playing.

Mercy walked toward the music, as if entranced, shaking off Abe's efforts to hold her back. She stopped, and Abe stopped beside her, a dozen feet from the stage at a position from which they could watch the performance without being seen by the audience.

She whispered to Abe, "Do you realize that Mercy never in her life saw a performance of a play, any performance at all, even by amateurs. I swear I can feel her excitement, as if I were her."

"Keep your head, please. Remember you're the one who preaches about risks and the need to exercise restraint."

"Shush! We'll miss the prologue."

A few minutes later, Abe whispered, "Good God I recognize this play. I wrote it. Burgoyne wrote it. *The Heiress.* First performed in January 1786."

"That's when my friends John and Abigail Adams were in London. I wonder if they're here. I feel certain that they're here, that that's why we're here and now."

"Don't start talking like Cat."

"This is the opportunity of a lifetime, of Mercy Warren's lifetime."

After the play, Mercy wanted to linger, and Abe started to pull her away. He wasn't sure he could find the door they came in by among all the dressing-room doors in the basement. He had no idea what might happen to them or to this world if they were lost and stuck here.

Abe halted suddenly and Mercy stopped as well. Burgoyne was standing in the path to the basement stairs. He was talking to someone who had a pen and pad of paper in hand. "It will be a dazzling success, I'm sure. The hit of the season."

"Thank you for your kind words, I'm sure. And what paper do you represent, sir?"

"The St. James Chronicle, also known as The British Evening Post."

"Ah, the Post, yes, the Post. Good day to you, sir." He shook the reporter's hand and turned to join a young woman and four small children who were impatiently waiting for him.

But he was intercepted by someone else who looked vaguely familiar and seemed determined to speak to him. This man was short and roundish and wore his clothes in a colonial manner, with a defiant flair, like they had been lived in for days rather than brushed and ironed each night, as if to say he didn't care what people thought of how he was dressed. He was carrying a large envelope.

"Have we met, sir?" asked Burgoyne, shaking hands with the ease and confidence of a politician.

"Adams. John Adams. I have seen you at receptions before, but I've never had the pleasure of meeting you."

"Adams? The American?"

"Yes, General, the ambassador."

"And what can I do for you, sir? Is this in an official capacity? The war ended three years ago. Surely the terms of my parole are no longer in question?" he chuckled.

"I was hoping to speak to you unofficially, having enjoyed your play and wanting to help a playwright friend of mine from home." He tried to hand Burgoyne the envelope, but Burgoyne backed away and tried to ignore the gesture. "Could you take a look at this or have one of your secretaries look at it? It's an American play entitled *The Group*."

"And how long a run did it have in New York?" asked Burgoyne, still not taking the envelope.

"It has not yet been performed in New York."

"Then where has it been performed?"

"Nowhere. No yet. The author is a lady from Massachusetts, where play performances are not allowed by law. That's a holdover from Puritan days."

"And she sends her play all the way to London where no one knows her rather than try it in her own country? And, without the benefit of performances, how could she have fine-tuned it for the professional stage?"

"I must admit that I do not know. To the best of my knowledge she has never seen any performance of any play, much less her own."

"This is absurd, my dear sir, absurd. Hardly worth the time of my secretary much less me."

"But she so hoped I could put this in your hands or the hands Sheridan or even Sarah Siddons. Perhaps you could pass it to one or the other of them? They are your friends I've heard."

"Friends, yes. But one does not waste the time of friends. That's what it means to be friends—to respect one another's time. Enough, sir. I'm sorry I can't help you. As you know I have the highest respect for your fledgling republic."

38 ~ The Nudge of Fate

"Selfish and petty," concluded Cat at the post-mortem in the activity room. "You insist that I not go, and you waste an opportunity to walk between centuries, for personal business, personal thrills and entertainment."

"Personal? You mean now there's no difference between me and the historical Mercy Warren? And what suits her, what matters to her, what's personal for her is personal for me?"

"It appears that that's what this has come down to. Not the high and mighty fate of the world or of multiple alternate worlds, just you wanting to see a play and get a play of yours produced. You should be ashamed of yourself. And the risk you took for that, plunging completely into that world. If you had been seen, if you had been recognized as out-of-place, as visitors from another time ... and all for such a petty purpose."

"No one noticed us," Mercy defended herself. "We wore masks, as many in the audience did. That was the fashion. We risked little. It was only a tiny change that my other self sought, and it would have meant so much to her. It could be the high point of her life. She had never done anything just for herself, always for others."

"Listen to yourself. Talking as if someone who has been dead for over two hundred years still has hopes and disappointments, that what happens now could matter to her. And you call me mystical?"

"You know what I mean. As Macaulay, you endured the same restrictions, the same sort of prejudice. Why even Adams, whom Mercy considered a close friend and ally, didn't believe that any woman could be a writer of true merit in competition with men. Women should stay in their place and do what they do best—manage the household, raise the children, deal with social events, support their husbands. If I could reach back to the past and give her a helping hand, help her get the recognition and support she deserved, of course I would. And, yes, it would feel like I was doing it for myself, but not just for myself. It would not be selfish in the sense that you mean."

"So, you've done a flip-flop. Now I'm the one advocating caution, while you're tempted to meddle with the stream of the past? Haven't we had enough of this now? I, for one, want to back off. When the most rational and level-headed and up-tight of us takes a risk like that for nothing, as if she were taken over by a spirit from the past and doing that person's bidding, we can't trust ourselves anymore. I certainly wouldn't trust myself. Let's get rid of these clothes, stop drinking this enchanted wine, stop using these silly Jemmie-names, and try to return to the lives we were living before. Forget the cellar and the doors and stepping into the past. Let the unknown stay unknown. And let's live the lives that we have for however much time we have left to us."

"No," insisted Mercy. "There's one more, at least one more."

"One more random stroll in the past? One more massive risk?"

"This one isn't random."

"And how could that be the case? Now you think you know what's behind those doors?"

"The first door we went through took us to Boston on September 5, 1769, the very day that James Otis was bashed in the head by a British agent and suffered permanent brain damage. The very day. That wasn't random. You have said that we are meant to do something, that all this strangeness has a purpose. Well, okay. If there's anything we're supposed to do, it's to save Jemmie on that very day in that very place."

"Now you're the one speaking nonsense. Even if you could save James Otis then, that wouldn't help your brother now. Stopping him from getting hit on the head, would not, could not, undo your brother getting struck by lightning in our era."

"We'll see. We'll see. We can and should do everything possible to save Jemmie. And if he's saved then, he may be saved now. I feel it in my gut. He will be restored to his self, to the brother I knew and loved as a child. My sane and brilliant, creative and deep-thinking brother. If I do this for him back there, he won't be struck by lightning centuries later. This is what I'm meant to do. Not for myself—for him."

"Stop," Cat shouted after them.

"What now?" asked Mercy, halting, but jogging in place, like a runner impatient to get going again.

"No, go ahead," Cat conceded. "Anything I'd say won't make a difference, if it could make a difference, I wouldn't be able to say it."

Mercy leaned against the way, doing stretching exercises. "Out with it. What now?"

"My thinking has evolved, and I don't like the drift of it. I'd prefer to stay my old self, the staunch republican, the firm believer in free will. But that's not where my head is now. It's as if something were nudging me this way, then that way, gently, unobtrusively. Sometimes I believe that what happens is under our control. Other times everything seems random. But it's neither. Rather, we're prompted and encouraged to go this way, then that. Why does this happen? What could be doing the nudging and why?

"Is this attitude of mine a symptom of moral callousness?" Cat asked herself aloud. "Is it a way to evade responsibility for doing what we damn well know we shouldn't? Or is that how we are given the illusion of free will when, in fact, we're controlled by forces beyond our ken.

"And on the rare occasion when we can't bring ourselves to do what we must do, maybe we repeat the same scene, like in the movie *Groundhog Day*, until finally we respond to the nudge and decide to do what we were supposed to do all along.

"Maybe that array of tunnels with doors leading to different times and places is the illusion of free will writ large. We're presented with what looks like the opportunity to catastrophically change everything, when, in fact, we'll be nudged to leave events unchanged.

"And is it only us here, in these extraordinary circumstances, who are subject to this nudging? Or is that the norm of human life—how we convince ourselves that we have free will while doing what we're fated to do?

"The direction of history isn't random and subject to the whims of everyone on Earth doing what they feel like doing. Nor can it be easily changed by inept time travelers. It is what it is and was predetermined. It was written before it happened, and we're just actors playing the parts we were given. Go or don't go. You risk nothing either way. What must happen will happen. Bon voyage."

39 ~ Jemmie's Moment

Before they set out, Abe took another look at the history of that event in the library. On the evening of September 5, 1769, James Otis, as was his habit, entered the British Coffee House at 66 State Street, a tenth of a mile, just two minutes by foot, from Faneuil Hall. There he saw his bitter enemy, John Robinson of the American Board of Customs Commissioners, a symbol of Britain's taxation policies. Otis had relentlessly hammered away at Robinson in newspaper articles. When Otis entered the coffee house, Robinson rushed at him and grabbed him by the nose. The lights went out, and Robinson struck him repeatedly with a heavy cane.

"How are you going to find him?" Abe asked Mercy.

She shrugged, then led the way with the flashlight, as they advanced through the dark and difficult tunnel. Abe kept a tight grip on her upper arm, to slow her anxious pace so he could keep up with her.

When they reached the door they had marked on their last excursion, she pushed his hand aside and ran in.

She jostled her way through the crowd in the tavern and dashed into the street, before she yelled back at Abe, showing no concern at all that the people around her could hear her and might consider her behavior bizarre, "I feel him in me. I'm drawn to him. I can't possibly miss him."

Abe followed as quickly as he could, without knocking people over.

He lost sight of her. But from the map of old Boston he had studied in the library, he knew the way to 66 State Street, so that's where he ran.

A block away from the Coffee House, he spotted them, standing in the middle of the street together. Mercy was talking to James Otis directly, her hands on his shoulders, her face in his face, lecturing him like a mother might lecture a teenage son who refused to obey her.

"Do you not understand? Is the English you speak in this day so very different from mine that this is not clear to you? Do I have to thee-and-thou to get this through? Robinson is in there. He is waiting for you. He is furious with you over your latest article. He intends to attack you with his cane. He will bash you on the head, and you will never be the same again. You will be a mental cripple for the rest of your life."

"And how didst thou get here, Mercy? I thought thou wert in Plymouth. Thou never toldst me thou planned to come to Boston. And where is James? He would never allow thee to walk the city streets alone."

"Listen to me. Your life depends on it."

"This is most extraordinary, most unaccountable. This is not like thee at all. Of course thou art my sister. Thou hast no twin. But thou wouldst never act like this, so irrational and so insistent, and talking nonsense, as if thou couldst prophesy the future."

"Yes, I am your sister. But at the same time, I am someone like her two hundred and fifty years in the future."

He laughed. "What hast thou been drinking? That's not thy nature. And certainly, thou wouldst not parade about in a public street under the influence."

"Please, Jemmie. Please listen to me!"

"Compose thyself, my dear. There's no reason to make a public scene. I'm a well-known figure in this city. People will take notice, and my enemies will find some way to mock me and rebut my arguments with foolery in the newspapers. Here's a bench, let's sit down for a moment, but no more than a moment. I have a hankering, a strong hankering to get me to that place of refreshment for I have a strong thirst, as strong a thirst as I have ever endured, strange though that be."

He sat down and patted the space beside him for her to join him.

"I shall indulge thee, to help calm thy spirits. I shall give thee time to get hold of thyself. Thou saidst that this Robinson rascal would bash me on the head in a public place, doing me grievous harm in front of witnesses. And he would get away with such an assault? And would there be no repercussions? Is that what this world is coming to?"

"He won't get away with it. You can be sure of that. It will be well known. There will be a public outcry. You will become a public martyr. You will become a lightning rod."

"Ben Franklin's invention? Brilliant man. I would so much like to meet him. And I should get one of those for myself and one for thee as well to protect thy home in Plymouth."

"I mean that as a metaphor, you blockhead."

"Blockhead?" he chuckled. "Thou art far out of sorts."

"It's not just you I'm talking about. It's the consequences, the long-range unintended consequences."

"And what are those consequences? From thy vast wisdom of what unfolds after this day, this blessed warm September day, tell me what happens."

"You become a symbol of dissent and rebellion. Your teachings about no taxation without representation spread not only in Massachusetts, but throughout the colonies. The general discontent and uneasiness and feelings of injustice become focused and lead to action."

"What action?"

"The Boston Tea Party."

"A tea party? How momentous. How earth-shattering. How proud that makes me, to think that people will gather and drink tea in remembrance of me and what was done to me."

"No, it was a protest. No, it will be a protest. Four years from now, colonists, Bostonians, will dump hundreds of chests of British tea into the harbor to protest British taxes."

"Why that would be a huge financial loss to whoever owned it."

"Indeed, Jemmie, nearly ten thousand pounds in your money, and nearly two million in mine."

"And thy money and my money are different? Maybe thou art the one who has been bashed in the head and is confused."

"Listen to me."

"Oh, I am listening, my dear, I am. This is most amusing. Whatever it is that has brought this madness on, and I do hope and believe it is temporary."

"The British will continue to provoke, will keep treating the colonists—"

"Us, my dear. We are the colonists. Do not talk as if thou wert somehow different. Speak precisely please. As a lawyer, I am trained in speaking precisely, and I always encourage thee to do the same. It's a discipline that is good for the functioning of the brain."

"Treating us, then, if you must, treating us as servants or as slaves, rather than as citizens with rights. And the people will rise up in rebellion. There will be fighting at Concord and at Lexington. There will be a full-fledged battle on Breed's Hill, the Battle of Bunker Hill. And the colonies, I mean *we*, will assemble a Congress and raise an army and declare independence, and fight and win a war, and become the United States of America, which will become the home of liberty and human rights and also the most powerful nation on Earth."

"All this from someone bashing me on the head? The consequences do not sound bad, not bad at all."

"I didn't mean it that way. I was trying to convince you not to go into that coffee house, not to let yourself be maimed like that."

"Thou hast an interesting debating style, my dear. If I believed thee, if I had any reason to believe that thou art a being from the future, that thou hast come here to tell me what is about to happen and what will happen after that, I would race across the street, go into that coffee house and welcome that head bashing, welcome becoming a martyr for such a cause, welcome becoming a small part of that magnificent advance for mankind. What a small price to pay. If only I could believe."

Then he stopped short, a look of panic in his eyes. "What is that?" he asked, pointing to an object tucked into the belt around her waist.

Mercy took it out. It was the flashlight. She had forgotten that she had put it there. Without thinking, she pushed the button that turned it on, then turned it off, then on again.

"It's true," he shouted. "Everything thou saidst is true. Wish me well, my love, my sis. And may the Lord have mercy on me."

He raced across the street, and before Abe had a chance to lift Mercy to her feet and give her support in her fit of sobbing, they heard a brawl erupting in the coffee house.

Storm clouds suddenly formed in what had been a calm, clear, sunset sky.

Mercy flipped the flashlight on and off, over and over again, without realizing she was doing so. Someone in the crowd that was gathering to check on the riot in the coffee house saw the flashlight and screamed and pointed. Others turned and looked and advanced toward her. She panicked, dropped the flashlight, took Abe's hand, and ran back toward Faneuil Hall

A torrent of rain fell, so hard they couldn't see their feet. But their path was straight and short. They could find Faneuil Hall even if they couldn't see it.

Mercy realized that their clothes were soaked and muddy, probably crawling with microbes from the garbage and the shit of horse and the shit of people, in the open sewers that were the streets of Boston in 1769.

They didn't have to worry about pursuers in this downpour, but they couldn't go back to the twenty-first century in these clothes. And they couldn't go back with their bodies filthy as well.

They could thank the rain for saving them from the angry mob, and they could thank it, too, for what it was doing to wash them. This was meant to be, thought Mercy, meant to happen just as it was happening.

"Strip," she yelled at Abe. She did, and he did, one piece at a time, as they kept going toward Faneuil Hall. No one saw them, because the rain was so intense. And when they walked through the main entrance to Faneuil Hall, no one took notice of them. And when they shouldered their way through the tavern, they didn't feel the touch of the people they were squeezing past, and no one reacted to their nakedness or their brusque rude passage. They reached the door, their door, the time-door, and passed through it, and shut it.

40 ~ Escape from Arcadia

Complete darkness. They had no flashlight.

They stubbed their toes and tripped time after time, scraping knees and elbows. Where the tunnel forked, their feet found the rocks that they had used to mark the way.

In the wine cellar, they chugged one bottle after another, then collapsed on the dirt floor.

No. That didn't happen. The drinking. They wouldn't stop for that. That was a dream.

Abe woke up in a dark room, in a bed with metal rails, with his arms strapped to the rails. A prisoner.

This was another dream, but who was doing the dreaming? Was it Abe alone? Or was Mercy having the same dreams?

Abe woke again and realized that he was being lifted from a bed to a wheelchair, then rolled down a hallway crowded with other wheelchairs occupied by old folks staring off into space.

He woke again. Mercy was groggy in a wheelchair beside his. Belle was in a wheelchair beside her. And Dick, beside her, was waving his left hand and moving his lips in time to music.

The music was a hymn being played by the player piano. Cat, Aphra, Nell, Fanny, and Jemmie sang,

"Oh God our help in ages past,

"Our hope for years to come,

"Our shelter from the stormy blast,

"And our eternal Home."

"Jemmie?" asked Abe. "How is Jemmie?"

"Jemmie is Jemmie. Same old Jemmie," answered Cat. "And a damn good thing, too. He saved you guys. He woke up in the middle of the night, sensing something was wrong. He was about to open the door and race to the lobby stark naked. But we stopped him and dressed him, before letting him go. When he got to the lobby, he jumped up and down trying to get the night guard at the front desk to look at the monitors with the video feeds from the back lawn. You and Mercy were both naked, lying in the snow. Lord only knows how long you could have lasted like that. The guard sounded the alarm. Orderlies fetched you. Margaret had you taken to the Alzheimer's wing where she had you strapped down until the medical staff could evaluate you.

"Meanwhile, I got a padlock of my own, one that I have a key for, and used it to replace the one on the cellar door. Whatever happened, I wanted to make sure we still had access to the basement and its passageways."

"What happened?" asked Abe.

"I was hoping you'd tell us. The administration has no idea how you got outside. The doors are all locked and alarmed at night. Surveillance video footage from that night didn't show you until you appeared, unconscious and naked, on the snow. The snow is old and encrusted so it doesn't show footprints. If it hadn't been for Jemmie—"

"Jemmie?" Mercy woke up asking, "How is Jemmie?"

Jemmie snapped to attention and saluted in child-like fashion, "James Otis, reporting for duty, ma'am."

"What did you dream, Mercy?" asked Abe.

"Nothing. Nothing that I remember. That was the first dreamless sleep I've had in months. And I have no urge to go back, no sense of unfinished business"

Cat smiled, "That's good news. Maybe whatever you did was what you needed to do. Maybe this is over."

"And nothing has changed with Jemmie?" asked Mercy.

"Nothing aside from his concern for you and Abe once you were found and brought in. Did you *save* him as you planned?"

"We could have. I told him what was going to happen, hoping he'd stop it from happening, but he chose to bring it on himself. Knowing the consequences, he was willing to sacrifice himself. While the original act was random, not of his own doing, the second time around it was his choice, a moral statement, placing the good of the country above his personal interests."

"Same act, different meaning," Cat concluded.

"Precisely."

"So, you did change something important, but without having an impact on subsequent events."

"I can't say that's what I intended to do, but that's what happened."

"We know you used the tunnel again, as planned. When I replaced the lock, the old one was open. So how the hell did the two of you end up naked, outside in the snow?"

"We lost the flashlight, probably left it in 1769 to be discovered as an object of wonder," explained Abe. "In short order, the batteries will die out, and it will be nothing more than a lump of plastic and metal, among people who have never seen plastic, much less an electrical device. With no practical purpose, it'll probably end up in a rubbish heap."

"What's so important about the flashlight?" asked Cat.

"Without it, we were in total darkness," Abe continued. "We couldn't find the door by which we had entered the tunnel. We wandered for hours. At least it felt like hours. Often, we stumbled and fell. I have no idea how we got out of there and how we ended up outside, back in the time and place where we started."

Mercy added, "Being naked was my choice. We had ventured into the city itself, a grimy smelly eighteenth-century city. We needed to get rid of our contaminated clothes, and we needed to do whatever we could to wash our bodies before heading back and spreading disease. It was raining hard, so hard we couldn't see our feet. So, we stripped and ran for it."

"And did you tell Margaret that?" asked Cat.

"I was foolish enough to try," Mercy admitted. "She tuned me out."

"She's convinced that the two of you are delusional, a risk to yourselves and others. She says you arrived with cuts on your feet and bruises, scrapes, and scratches on your legs. She had you put in the Alzheimer's wing and strapped to the bedrails. Doctors are supposed to evaluate you to determine if you should be moved to a hospital or a mental institution. If you're diagnosed with a memory disorder, they'll keep you here in the Alzheimer's wing, but there's no way they would let your return to your assisted-living apartments. She asked us if we had any idea what was going on with you, but we didn't tell her anything she didn't know already. She'd have never believed us. We'd have ended up on her list of crazies. I wasn't about to tell her about the tunnel—not that she would have believed me, but I feel that that is something special, almost sacred, and getting the authorities involved and poking around down there would jeopardize something extraordinary that we have been privileged to learn about.

"We've been pressuring Margaret to hold off and not make irreversible decisions about your apartments or your property. But even before the doctors have delivered an authoritative diagnosis, she has contacted your families. The kiddies will be arriving soon to deal with their naughty parents."

"How much time do we have?" asked Mercy.

"Why should that matter?" asked Cat. "Your fate now depends on doctors, kids, and bureaucrats. A perfect end to the story of your lives. There's nothing you or we can do about it."

"Does anybody here have a car?" asked Abe.

Cat volunteered, "I have a twenty-year old purple Dodge Caravan. It doesn't look like much, but it runs. You're welcome to it."

"Terrific, Cat. That's what we need," Abe affirmed. "Mercy, can you pick the lock and disable the alarm on the south door near the back parking lot?"

"That should be no problem."

"Then we'll make a run for it tonight, hopefully before the kids get here."

"But I have no money to speak of," objected Mercy. "What about you?"

"A couple of twenties. But nearly a thousand in a bank account I can tap into by ATM."

"And what are we going to do when that runs out?"

"Wine. We'll sell the wine. We'll sell it on eBay. It should be worth a bundle."

Mercy laughed. "Well, we may starve to death, but at least we'll be free and drunk and happy."

"Cat, Aphra, Fanny, and Nell, fill the van with wine from the cellar," Abe ordered. "There must be hundreds of bottles down there. Don't let anyone see you going to the basement. Be careful on the stairs. Take only a few bottles at a time. Strap them to your legs under your petticoats. And keep us here in the activity room past curfew. They won't know we're missing until bed-check starting at 9 p.m. In the meantime, we'll make a run for it."

"A run for it?" asked Cat. "In wheelchairs, you'll make a run for it?"

Abe stood up. "I don't need this damn thing for a few scratches on my legs." He smiled and sat back down. "We'll rest now to be ready to drive all night. In the meantime, the wheelchairs make a good diversion. And please fetch my antique clothes. I've gotten used to that get-up, and it would be fun to be dressed like that when we make our Bonnie-and-Clyde escape."

Jemmie stayed behind. The ladies didn't want him to go.

Abe and Mercy took turns at the wheel and drove all night. They spent the following day at a Holiday Inn north of Hartford. They used a computer in the hotel's lobby to research prices for old wine on eBay. There was nothing comparable. Then they did a general search and found that Sotheby's had sold at auction a bottle from 1810 for $40,000. The next day, they drove to New York and went straight to Sotheby's. They had 240 bottles. They sold the lot to Sotheby's for nearly five million dollars.

One rumor has it that they then went on a world cruise out of Fort Lauderdale, planning, as in their dream, to live on one ship after another for the rest of their lives.

According to another tale, they used the money they got from the wine sale to buy online from Walmart facsimiles of paper money from the time of the Revolution. This money was printed on antiqued parchment paper. With the technology of the day, it would be indistinguishable from originals. Then they drove to Boston, walked to Faneuil Hall, went down to the basement, and were never seen again.

In any case, they lived happily ever after, at least twice, and probably more times than that.

About the Author

Richard now lives in Milford, CT, where he writes fiction full-time. He worked for DEC, the minicomputer company, as writer and Internet Evangelist. He graduated from Yale with a major in English, went to Yale grad school in Comparative Literature and earned an MA in Comparative Literature from the U. of Mass. at Amherst. At Yale, he had creative writing courses with Robert Penn Warren and Joseph Heller. His personal web site is seltzerbooks.com. His Twitter account is @seltzerbooks

His published works include: The Name of Hero (historical novel), Ethiopia Through Russian Eyes (translation from Russian), The Lizard of Oz (satiric fantasy), and pioneering books about Internet business. Complete list at seltzerbooks.com/seltzer.html

ALL THINGS THAT MATTER PRESS

FOR MORE INFORMATION ON TITLES AVAILABLE FROM
ALL THINGS THAT MATTER PRESS, GO TO
http://allthingsthatmatterpress.com
or contact us at
allthingsthatmatterpress@gmail.com

**If you enjoyed this book, please post a review on Amazon.com
and your favorite social media sites.
Thank you!**

Made in the USA
Middletown, DE
07 March 2020